W9-BTI-271

HANGING WOMAN
CREEK

**Center Point
Large Print**

Also by Louis L'Amour
and available from Center Point Large Print:

The Ferguson Rifle
Showdown at Yellow Butte
Last Stand at Papago Wells
Trailing West: A Western Quartet
Big Medicine: A Western Quartet

**This Large Print Book carries the
Seal of Approval of N.A.V.H.**

HANGING WOMAN CREEK

LOUIS L'AMOUR

CENTER POINT PUBLISHING
THORNDIKE, MAINE

This Center Point Large Print edition
is published in the year 2010 by arrangement with
Bantam Dell, a division of Random House, Inc.

The text of this Large Print edition is unabridged.
In other aspects, this book may vary
from the original edition.
Printed in the United States of America
on permanent paper.
Set in 16-point Times New Roman type.

ISBN: 978-1-60285-640-0

Library of Congress Cataloging-in-Publication Data

L'Amour, Louis, 1908-1988.
  Hanging Woman Creek / Louis L'Amour. -- Center Point large print ed.
    p. cm.
  Originally published: New York : Bantam Books, 1964.
  ISBN 978-1-60285-640-0 (library binding : alk. paper)
  1. Large type books. I. Title.
  PS3523.A446H27 2010
  813'.54--dc22
2009030579

HANGING WOMAN CREEK

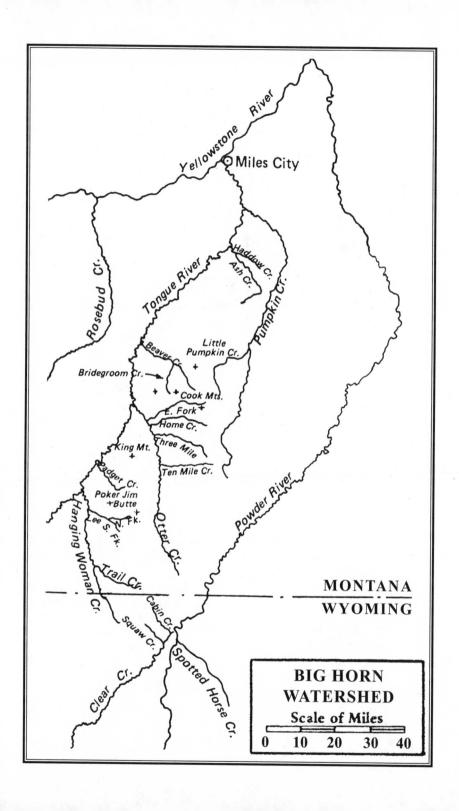

Yellowstone River

Rosebud Cr.

Miles City

Tongue River

Haddow Cr.

Ash Cr.

Pumpkin Cr.

Little Pumpkin Cr.

Beaver Cr.

Bridegroom Cr.

Cook Mts.

E. Fork

Home Cr.

Three Mile

King Mt.

Ten Mile Cr.

Badger Cr.

Poker Jim Butte

Lee S. Fk.

N. Fk.

Otter Cr.

Powder River

Hanging Woman Cr.

Trail Cr.

Cabin Cr.

MONTANA

WYOMING

Squaw Cr.

Spotted Horse Cr.

Clear Cr.

BIG HORN WATERSHED

Scale of Miles

0   10   20   30   40

Milk River
Missouri River
MONTANA
Butte
Musselshell R.
Virginia City
Yellowstone R.
Glendive
Medora
Jamestown
Fargo
Northern Pacific RR.
DAKOTA
TERRITORY
James R.
Detail Map
Deadwood
Black Hills
Badlands
DAHO
Hole-in-the-Wall
WYOMING
N. Platte
NEBRASKA
Cheyenne
S. Platte
Platte River
UTAH
ROCKY MOUNTAIN
Denver
COLORADO
Kit Carson
KANSAS

NORTHERN PLAINS
Scale of Miles
0   50   100 150 200

CHAPTER 1

IT WAS RAINING by the time we reached the railroad bridge. Evening was coming on, and the pelting rain was cold.

We dug in our heels and slid down the embankment to get under the bridge, where there was shelter of a sort. We built a fire, then huddled over it wondering what had become of our summer's wages.

Three of us were there, strangers until a few hours ago, now joined in the idea of going west. I'd be going home, or to as much of a home as I could lay claim to, being rootless as a tumbleweed, blowing on, resting here and there against this fence or that, but staying nowhere long. As for the others, I had no idea.

The black skeleton frame of the trestle danced in the wavering light from the fire, and from time to time the flames guttered and hissed as the wind blew down the draw, spattering us with cold drops from off the bridge.

Rustling around for wood reminded me of a winter I spent in Montana one time . . . at the Hartman & Liggett horse camp. No snow on the ground all winter long, only flurries from time to time, but cold. The ice froze rock-hard on the creek that year, and never broke until late spring.

Taking all in all, that had been a good winter.

The cabin was snug against the wind, the pot-bellied stove gave off almost too much heat, and there were old magazines and a couple of books lying around.

When not in a mind to read, I'd sit and ponder. Whilst only a youngster I had taken to rebuilding places in my mind, places I'd lived in or seen, and when I'd nothing else to do I would put a place together, every single thing in place, then bit by bit I'd recall the folks I'd known there and what was said—what we talked about, and the like. It gave me something to do, but no great respect for the high art of conversational talk.

When a man sets out to recall in detail as I did, he sets more to working than he's figured on, for he never looks at anything after that without thinking how he'll recall it in time to come. It also sets a man to thinking about himself, and when a man stands himself up to ponder at, he can't always be pleased at what he sees.

No working cowhand is going to get very far unless he's a hand to notice. Punching cows takes you over a lot of rough country, and pretty soon you get to know every draw, hill, or clump of brush. You notice the game trails and the springs, and where the cattle go for shelter, and a lot more besides. A man has to notice or he won't get very far at punching cows.

Back there at the Hartman & Liggett horse camp there'd always been a brown crock of baked beans, and I'd never had my fill of beans. Sitting there beside that hateful fire under the trestle with night coming on, I kept thinking back to that horse camp and those crocks of beans. They would be tasty, mighty tasty, right now.

That big colored boy, he looked at me and he said, "You look like you been in a fight."

"Here an' there," I said.

"You fight with the mitts?"

"Nobody ever showed me. I just fight the best way I know how."

"I've boxed," he said.

He was a big boy, maybe a year or two older than my twenty-six years, standing around six feet, and built strong. And he had good hands.

That was the first thing he said about me. "You got good hands." He doubled up my fist. "Flat across the knuckles. Stands shock better. You could punch, I think."

Puttering around, I fetched back a few more sticks. A branch or two, a few old sticks and such-like—anything to keep the fire going.

"When did you say that freight was due?" Van Bokkelen asked.

"Ten-twelve, if it's on time."

Van Bokkelen was a big blond man, raw-boned and with an uncurried look—shaggy hair and a broad, tough face, yet not bad-looking. He had small, ice-blue eyes, no more warmth in them than in the head of a nail.

11

Twelve hours before no one of us had known the others. We'd come together in jail, in the drunk tank. Only I'd been pulled in for fighting, and it wasn't the first time. Seemed like I was always being arrested for fighting. Not that I knew much about it, but I just naturally liked to fight.

The wind blew cold. Rain spattered over us, and I hitched the collar of my cloth suit-coat higher around my ears and stretched my hands toward the flames.

We were sheltered in part by a bank of drift sand; on our left ran a small stream. The rain was falling harder now, the gusts were more frequent.

"You got a place?" Eddie Holt, the colored boy, asked. "I mean, you got a place to go to?"

"I got no place, and never had no place except west." With a gesture I indicated my sacked-up saddle. "My home's been in the middle of that."

"You got to have a horse."

"You think so, do you? Sometimes I figure I've packed that saddle damn near as far as I've rode horses."

"I'd be damned if I'd pack it," Van Bokkelen said. "I'd steal a horse before I'd do that."

"It's been done," I admitted, not wanting to argue principle with a stranger over a friendly fire.

We listened to the rain, and hopefully listened for a train whistle, but it was a long while until train time and I was hungry as a springtime bear fresh out of hibernation.

"Maybe I could get me a riding job," Eddie suggested.

"There was a colored boy rode for an outfit I worked for down New Mexico way. He was a good hand. Can you ride?"

"I never rode for no cow outfit, but I rode in a Buffalo Bill Show." He grinned at me. "I was an Indian."

"You ain't the first," I said, and then added, "They tell me you really got to ride for Cody."

"I can ride. I can rope a little. But I never rode for no cow outfit."

"A man who can't live without working," Van Bokkelen scoffed, "is a fool. I'd see myself in hell before I'd eat dust behind a bunch of cows."

Well, I sat quiet, feeling the Old Ned coming up in me. All my life I've punched cows or worked hard for what little I'd had, and I didn't cotton to this stranger making me out a fool. Come to think of it, he didn't seem to be doing so well.

Eddie Holt, he sat quiet, too, and never said aye, yes, or no, and that seemed to be a good idea. This blond gent was a whole lot bigger than me, and my ribs and jaw were still sore from my last fight.

"You do what you're of a mind to," I said after a minute. "I'll punch cows."

"For thirty a month?" he sneered. "You boys come along with me and you'll be wearin' silk shirts and broadcloth. I could use two men like you."

Back up the line I heard a footstep splash in the

13

water. "Somebody comin'," I said, and turned my head to look. When I looked back Van Bokkelen was gone.

"Sit close," Eddie warned. "It's the law."

It sure was. There were four of them, four big men wearing slickers and armed with shotguns. They had spread out as they came up to the fire and they looked from one to the other of us.

"You!" The man I knew as the sheriff gestured with his shotgun. "Stand up!" He came up to me. "You armed?"

"I owned a Winchester one time," I said. "Never had no use for a hand gun."

He went over me with as smooth and knowing a frisk as ever I got, then did the same for Eddie.

"You haven't even got a knife? Or a razor?"

Eddie lifted his big hands. "Never had use for anything but these," he said.

The sheriff looked around at a narrow-faced, red-haired man. "Didn't you say there were three of them? You had three of them, you said."

"That's right. They didn't come together, but they left together. The black boy there, he was straight vag. Loafing around, no visible means of support. We gave him overnight in jail and a floater.

"The one in the broad hat, he got into a fight with Salty Breakenridge over to Ryan's. They busted up the place."

The sheriff looked at me with respect. "With Salty? I saw him. I figured it had to be a bigger man than you. What do you weigh, puncher?"

"Hundred and seventy," I said. "I never seen size makes too much difference." Then kind of grudgingly I had to acknowledge, "Although that there Salty . . . I'd say he was a fair hand."

The sheriff chuckled. "Yes, I'd say that. Nobody ever whipped him before."

He kicked the sack containing my gear. "What's in that?"

"Saddle. I'm headed west."

"How'd you come east? Trainload of cattle?"

"Uh-huh."

The quiet man with the gray eyes had said nothing up to then, but he had been looking around. "Where's the other one?" he asked. "The big blond man?"

"Ain't seen him," I said, "only once since we left jail. He was headin' for Ryan's and a drink." I grinned at them. "I figured I'd no business goin' back there."

They just looked at me, and then the quiet man said, "Don't cover for him, boys. He isn't worth it. That's a bad man."

"I wouldn't know," I said, "but you had him in jail—why didn't you keep him?"

The sheriff spat. "Because we didn't know who he was. Like damn fools we let him go. Then Fargo here, he got to thinking about an old reward poster. There's a reward on that man . . . dead or alive. He's wanted for murder."

Eddie, he never even looked at me.

"How much?" I said, for I was curious.

"Five thousand."

Hell, I never seen that much money in my whole lifetime. You don't see much, working for thirty a month and found. It was a lucky thing when I put forty saved dollars into a saddle.

Fargo looked at me. "What's your name, cowpuncher?"

"Pike," I said, "Barnabas Pike. Some places they call me Pronto."

"Pronto? Because you're fast?"

Me, I grinned at him. "Maybe because I swing too quick," I said. "I got a mean temper when I'm riled, but it ain't always that. I never had much fun . . . except fightin'."

"I can believe it," the sheriff said. "I saw Salty Breakenridge after."

They poked around a little, stared off down the stream bed, and then they started off. Only Fargo lingered. He kicked at the ground where Van Bokkelen had sat. "Five thousand," he said, "is a lot of money."

"Mister," I said, "I seen that gent in jail and I didn't cotton to him, but I never sold anybody out yet, and I ain't about to start."

"I thought you'd be that way," Fargo said quietly, "but don't tangle with that man. You leave him alone, cowpuncher. He's bad medicine."

"You been west," I said.

"A time or two," he said. "And maybe again."

Then he walked off after the others, and we said nothing, Eddie Holt and me, watching them go.

Finally Eddie picked up sticks and added them to the fire. "Murder," he said—"that's bad. I wonder who he killed?"

"He's full of mean," I said. "I could see it in him."

I looked at Eddie. "You goin' any place particular? If you ain't, come along with me. Two can starve as free as one, and if I get a ridin' job I'll speak for you."

"I take that kindly," he said.

The fire was warm; the wind had gone down and the rain had about stopped. There was still the sound of the big drops falling off the trestle.

A long time we sat quiet, and me wishing I could catch some shut-eye, but little time remained if we were going to catch that drag. I kept squatting there thinking about how I wished there'd be an empty on that train. I'd never liked riding freights unless there was an empty.

"We're partners, Pronto?" Eddie said.

"Why not?" I said, and then the train whistled far off.

We got up and Eddie kicked out the fire mostly, and then scooped water from the creek with an old can and poured it over what was left to put it out. Then we struggled up to the trestle together.

The train slowed up along here, with a good grade ahead, and a man could take it moving.

"Can you make it? Totin' that saddle?"

"You watch me."

We let a dozen cars go by, and then Eddie saw an open door as it passed a red light on a switch, and called out to me. He was a fast man, making the run easy and swinging up, and he caught my saddle as I swung it at the opening. Me, I caught the edge of the floor and hauled myself up, the ground slipping away behind me.

Long after Eddie had rolled up in some paper he found at one end of the car, I sat there by the open door, a-looking out at the country. Here and there we flipped past lonely farms with lights in the windows . . . one time there was a man walking to-ward the house with a lantern and a milk pail, and a dog barking at the train.

"Dirt farmers," I sneered. "Home guards!" But away down inside I wasn't sneering at all. That man was going into his own house to set down to his supper at his own table, with his kinfolk around him.

And me? All I had was a lonesome whistle sound as the train bent around a curve, the distant glow of the firebox, and somewhere down the line a flea-bitten cow pony, and a chuck wagon for home.

CHAPTER 2

WHEN I WOKE up it was daylight and the train was bumping along at a good pace. Walking to the door, I could see patches of woods, a stream and miles of wheat fields slipping by.

Eddie sat up. "That right, what you said? We're partners?"

"Sure."

"Where all we goin'?"

"West . . . I dunno. Maybe Miles City . . . Medora. First place that looks likely."

"I could eat. Boy, but I could eat!"

"You an' me," I said.

"You been punchin' cows a long time?"

"Uh-huh. Since I was twelve. Worked along with my brother until he got killed, then on my own for the BB. My brother was never no hand with a gun, but he surely figured he was. Finally one time he braced a cow-town marshal."

The train was slowing a little. Leaning out of the door, I could see the long sweep of the cars ahead as they rounded a curve and started up a steep grade.

"I never blamed that marshal. My brother was dead set on proving himself a fast man. The marshal told him to go home and sleep it off, but Alex, he just went ahead and dragged iron."

"You see it?"

"Sure. That marshal, he walked over and looked at the body, and then he looked up at me, an' he said, 'Boy, I'd no choice. I hope you don't hold that again' me.'

" 'He was huntin' you,' I said, 'an' I tried to talk him out of it, but he sure had a streak of mule in him. Figured he was fast.'

" 'He wasn't fast, son. He wasn't even close.' "

We sat down in the boxcar door and dangled our legs. The sun was warm and pleasant. You could smell coal smoke from the engine, and that hot dry smell you get from ripening grain fields. They'd be shucking wheat in no time at all, but I'd had my fill of that, even though it paid better than punching. I never hunted no kind of work a man couldn't do from the back of a horse.

"Comin' to a town," Eddie said.

"Uh-huh."

"Seems to me you could get you a pass. I mean on this railroad. They tell me when a man ships cattle or rides with cattle, the railroad will give him a pass back home."

"You heard it right. On'y I didn't take to that new clerk back in Chicago. The one I used to know, he was all right. This one looks down his nose at a man . . . nobody does that to Barney Pike."

Suddenly footsteps drummed on the car top, and then a face leaned over, grinning. It was Van Bokkelen. He turned around, lowered his feet, then his full length, and, swinging by his hands he swung in and dropped to the floor of the car beside us.

"You could get killed that way," I said.

He chuckled. "My number's not up." There was a hard, reckless light in his eyes that I did not like. Maybe because they were also lighted with contempt. The way I figure it, a man has no right to hold anybody or anything in contempt . . . especially the odds. From time to time I'd seen a few men die, and I couldn't bring myself to think there was any special providence looking out for any of us.

Seems to me we work out our destinies subject to a lot of accident, incident, and whim. The men I'd seen die, died mostly because they were in the wrong place at the wrong time, and the kind of men they were mattered not in the least. The good seemed to go as easily as the bad, the brave as quickly as the cowards.

As for me, I did what I had to do, what I believed I should do, and tried not to take any unnecessary chances. Here and there I'd seen more than one man die showing how brave he was, or doing something he was dared to do . . . which didn't make sense any way you looked at it.

"That law back there," Van Bokkelen asked, "he ask about me?"

"Uh-huh."

"What did he say?"

"Nothin' much. On'y they seemed anxious to lay

hands on you. If I was you," I added, "I'd fight shy of places. And we're comin' into a town now."

"You call that a town?" he sneered. "That's nothing but a wide spot in the road. The town clown in a place like that won't worry me."

The "town clown" . . . I'd heard that name given to small-town peace officers before, but not by me. More often than not the constable or marshal in those little towns is a good enough sort if you give him a chance, and often he's mighty salty when pushed. Right then I decided the further we stayed away from Van Bokkelen, the better. He was a trouble-hunter, and Boot Hill graveyards were filled with his kind.

"They don't bother me." He slapped his waistband. "I'm packing the difference."

Why do all those would-be toughs talk like echoes of each other? How many times had I heard such talk since I was a kid, knocking around? And each one of them figures he's got a patent on luck and brains. They live like animals in their hideouts, coming out every once in a while, and the rest of the time hiding from the law and bragging about all they plan to do. And then, like the James-Younger gang, they run into a bunch of farmers and small-town businessmen and get shot to doll rags.

"That gun you're packin'," I told him, "is the handle that will open a grave for you on Boot Hill."

Eddie Holt got up. "Pronto, let's unload and hunt us some grub."

Van Bokkelen chuckled. "You boys on your uppers? Don't be damn fools. Stick with me and you'll be rollin' in money."

"You're ridin' the same train we are," I said.

An ugly light came into his eyes. "What I'm doing here is my own business, and business is good." He brought a roll of bills from his pocket. "How about that?"

"Eddie, there's a house with a woodpile and two axes," I said. "Let's you and me see if we can earn our breakfast."

Eddie dropped to the roadbed, ran a few steps, then walked back to meet me. I tossed my saddle out into the weeds, and dropped off myself.

The last I heard was Van Bokkelen saying, "A couple of finks! Just plain bums!"

"I don't like that man," Eddie said. "There's trouble in him."

He waited by the woodpile while I walked up to the house and rapped on the door. A stout Irish woman looked at Eddie and then at my sack. "What's in that?" she asked.

"My saddle, ma'am. I'm a rider, but right this minute I'm ridin' a two-day hunger. There's a pair of axes, and we were wondering if we could earn a meal."

"Well, now, you're a couple of stout lads. You heft those axes a while and I'll be makin' up me mind."

We'd worked only a few minutes when she came to the door. "Come off it, now!" she called. "Pat'll be home for his supper, and if he found me makin' you work for a meal he'd take the stick to me."

She produced two big plates piled high with ham hocks, mashed potatoes, and corn on the cob, and set them down on the stoop. "If that's not enough, rap on the door. Himself is a healthy eater, and I know he'd make way with twice the lot."

We sat down by the food, and she placed a pitcher of cold milk besides us and went back inside.

"There's good people wherever you go," Eddie said. "She didn't even comment that I was a black man."

"Could be she didn't notice," I said.

If her Pat was a healthy eater we'd no idea of putting the man to shame, so after a bit we knocked on the door and she filled our plates again, then brought a paper sack to the door. It was a peck sack, and packed to the top.

"Here's a bit to take along," she said, "and there's a mite of coffee there if you can find somewhat to make it in."

"Thank you, ma'am," I said. "Thank you, indeed."

"Obliged," Eddie said.

"It's been said that hoboes mark the gates of houses where they'll be fed. Is it true, then?"

"Ma'am, I've no idea. Only I shall remember

this place as the home of the fairest flower of Old Ireland. You're the picture of loveliness, ma'am."

"Oh, g'long with you! You've had your bait. Now take yourselves off!"

We slept the night in another empty boxcar, listening to the creaking of the car as it rounded curves, the bumping as the train rolled over the tracks. We had seen no more of Van Bokkelen, and I was sure he had left the town before us, and I was pleased at that.

"Where do we stop next?" Eddie asked. "I've never ridden the N.P. before."

"Jimtown, I guess. If we can pick up a meal there, we can ride on to Miles City, with a little tightening of the belt."

"That's a far piece," Eddie objected, "and I'm a man likes to eat."

The train rumbled along, accompanied by whistles now and then as it neared some road crossing. The country we were passing through was broken into wheat fields . . . miles of them . . . and sometimes there were stretches of pasture-land. It was a glaciated region of rolling prairies with occasional low hills and small lakes or sloughs, their fringes lined with cattails. The only trees were those along the streams, or freshly planted ones near farmhouses or villages.

When the freight slowed down before coming into the station at Jimtown, we dropped off and headed for Main Street. This was my second time in the town, and I saw that it had changed some.

"I was shy of fourteen," I told Eddie, "and came riding in here on the first train over the road. The BB outfit had driven some cattle from Texas to Abilene, then shipped them to Chicago, and I'd gone along.

"The boss, he decided to have a look at the Dakota grass, so he rode that first train west with a few horses and a couple of hands. He took me along to feed the stock."

"Nothing much here then, I reckon," Eddie commented. "Ain't much now."

"Mostly tents then," I said. "Now they've got hotels and everything."

It was in my mind to look around for a man I'd known as a boy in Fargo-in-the-Timber. Back in those days that was the roughest place a man could find, and it stayed rough until Custer's soldiers cleaned it out. Jack O'Niel had killed three of the soldiers before they moved in to get him.

This friend of mine was one of the BB cowboys who decided to stay in Dakota, like I had, and we stayed together in Fargo-in-the-Timber. There was a Fargo-on-the-Prairie, too, but that was mostly decent folks, but not so exciting to me as Fargo-in-the-Timber.

This man I knew, he was wise enough to decide we should leave Fargo-in-the-Timber after Jack O'Niel killed those soldiers. He had known the Seventh Cavalry down in Kansas, and they weren't likely to stand by when some of their outfit had been killed. We had nothing to do with it, but my friend taught me a good lesson then. "Stay away from trouble," he told me. "It's the innocent bystanders who get hurt."

So we went west to the end of the line on the James River . . . to Jamestown, which everybody called Jimtown. It was built in a valley where the Pipestem River flowed into the James, and there were a few soldiers stationed there when we first came.

Now there were no uniforms about, and small as the place was, it looked prosperous.

"If we find this friend of yours," Eddie asked, "will he stake us to a feed?"

"That's my guess," I said; "and if he's around I know how to find him. I'll hunt up a drugstore. Tom Gatty never could pass up a drugstore. I never knew a man who had so many ailments. He told me he never knew how sick he was until he was snowed in one winter with a *Home Medical Advisor*, and read it cover to cover. If it hadn't been for that book, he might have lived a long life in bad health without knowing it."

We found a drugstore, and while Eddie watched my saddle on the street, I went in the store. "I'm hunting a man named Tom Gatty," I said.

"Three like him, and I wouldn't need anybody else for customers," the druggist said. "He's the strongest dying man I ever knew, but you've come too late. He went west . . . Medora, I think."

"Just my luck," I said.

The man came from behind the counter. "You might learn something from Duster Wyman. He handles Gatty's local business."

The Gatty I knew had no head for business, nor for poker, either, when it came to that. "Last time I saw him he was punching cows," I said. "We worked for the same outfit."

"That must have been several years ago. Mr. Gatty has been shipping cattle, trading in horses and mules. He's done very well, I believe."

We found the Duster loafing in front of a saloon, and when I told him I was hunting Tom Gatty he got up carefully, and looked me over, and then looked Eddie over, too.

"Just what do you want with him?" The Duster was carrying a gun, tucked back of his belt, under his coat. A rough guess told me that Duster Wyman was a pretty salty character; and if Gatty was trading in horses, mules, and cattle they must have some fancy work for brands. Come to think of it, Tom Gatty used to brag he could write a Spencerian hand with a cinch ring, so I began to understand some of the phases of his business.

"As a matter of fact," I explained, "I was hunting a road stake. Me an' Eddie here, we're broke and headed for Miles City. Tom was an old friend of mine. In fact, we came to Dakota together."

"What did you say your name was?"

"Pike . . . they call me Pronto."

Well, his face cleared right up. He had been looking mighty suspicious until then. "Oh, sure! I've heard him speak of you."

He ran his hand down into his Levis and came up with a handful of silver dollars. He counted out ten of them. "You take this," he said. "I'll get it back from Tom."

"Where'll I find him?"

"Well, he moves around a good deal. Don't you go askin' for him. If you want to see him, look around Miles City. You stay around a while and he'll find you."

When we walked away from there, Eddie looked at the money with respect. "You got you some good friends," he said.

Me, I didn't say anything, because I was wondering why the Duster was so quick to hand out ten dollars and say Tom would pay him back. Tom Gatty never had much money, but the way I remembered him he was mighty poor pay. Of course, that could have been because he never had much. Maybe he was doing better now.

If he could afford having a man living around Jimtown like the Duster was, well, he was doing a lot better.

But why ship from here? Why not from Miles City itself?

We had ourselves a meal, and when we came out of the restaurant a man was standing on the curb. "Hello, Pike," he said.

It was that man Fargo that we'd last seen a couple of hundred miles east.

"I figured you'd settle in eastern Dakota, with a town named for you," I said.

"It wasn't named for me." He took some cigars from his pocket and offered them. "Smoke?"

It was a good cigar.

He took one himself and we all lit up. Then he said, "You're living good."

"We got a right."

"I was wondering how somebody broke enough to cut wood for a meal could suddenly pay cash for one."

"Look, mister, you ain't the law here. You want to start something, you keep poking that long nose into my business."

He chuckled. "You have the best of me there. I can't break yours. Somebody beat me to it."

Well, what could I do but laugh? My nose had been broken a couple of times. "The hell with it! You followin' us?"

"No. Just going west. Have you seen any more of Van Bokkelen?"

Odd thing. I'd been so busy thinking about Tom Gatty that I'd forgotten all about Van Bokkelen.

When I didn't say anything, Fargo glanced at his cigar and commented, "Pike, you strike me as an honest man. Maybe a hard one to get along with, but an honest one. So I don't want you to get in trouble."

"I been up the crick," I said, because I had. Most ways, I knew my way around.

"All right." He held out his hand. "Boys, my name is Jim Fargo—call me Jim. And if you ever want to talk about things, or if there's anything I can do, call on me."

We walked away and left him standing there, and when we had gone several blocks toward the west end of town where we would catch our freight going out, Eddie said to me, "He's a Pink, Pronto. That's a Pinkerton man."

And it made a lot of sense. . . . But who was he after? Van Bokkelen?

They had said Van Bokkelen was wanted for murder, and the Pinks usually only hunted train robbers or the like. I said as much.

"That Van Bokkelen, maybe he murdered a Pink," said Eddie.

CHAPTER 3

WE DROPPED OFF the freight before it reached Miles City station, and walked up Pacific Avenue.

"This here's a live town," I said to Eddie, "and it's purely cattle." But after a few steps I amended that. "Now, I better back off on that, for I should say this here is a *stock* town—there's folks around who favor sheep."

We turned off and went past the cat houses to

31

Main, and kept on to Charley Brown's saloon. A couple of Hat X punchers were loafing in front of the saloon, and one of them, seeing me packing that gear, commented, "Now lookit there. First time I ever seen Pronto when he had the saddle in the right place."

"Least I chase the steers," I said. "They don't chase me."

Dropping the saddle to the boardwalk, I dug into my pocket for the stub end of the cigar Fargo had given me. They eyed me whilst I lit up, making a great show of it to impress them with my prosperity.

"Eddie and me,"—I jerked my head to indicate my Negro partner—"are huntin' a business connection where we can invest our time and my saddle."

"You might try the Diamond R," one of the punchers said, grinning wickedly. "They always seemed ready to take you on."

"You can spread the word," I said solemnly, "those Diamond R bull-whackers are safe. I'm a *ree*formed man."

"Now, they'll be mighty relieved to hear you said that," the other puncher commented dryly. "Butch Hogan was around on'y last night, sayin' how dull it was with you out of town. There was nobody around to whip."

"He on'y whupped me once."

"Sure . . . you on'y tried him once. You stick around. You can have you another chance tonight."

"He still around over at John Chinnick's?"

They exchanged a glance. "You surely been gone. Chinnick left out of here one night . . . by special invite."

That was news, but not unexpected. Chinnick's saloon had been a long-time hangout for the wild bunch. If anything was going on, you could hear of it over to Chinnick's . . . if they knew you.

Big-Nose George and his crowd hung out there when they were in town, and come to think of it, Tom Gatty had a few friends in that outfit. But when I started to ask about Tom, something warned me to hold off. Tom an' me, we'd been friends, but never saddle partners.

We went into Charley Brown's and I led the way to the stove. Charley always kept a big pot of mulligan stew going on the stove, and you could help yourself. Eddie an' me, we couldn't afford to pass up a social invitation of that sort.

"That Butch Hogan," Eddie said, "did he whup you?"

"He did that, and good. He's big and he's fast, and much as I hate to admit it, he'll probably do it again."

"Then why fight him?"

Well, I just looked at Eddie, plainly surprised. "He whupped me, and when a man whups me once, he's got it to do again . . . and again, if need be, until either I whup him or he leaves the country. A couple of times," I added, "they've done just that. Maybe they just plain got tired of having me to whup every Saturday night."

"We get a job together," Eddie said, "we can box some. Get you in shape."

We ate for a while without talking, and then Eddie went on, "I boxed forty-seven times in the ring for money. I boxed Paddy Ryan before he was champion, and I boxed Charlie Mitchell over in England. I boxed Joe Goss, Dominick McCaffrey, and Joe Coburn."

Little as I knew about prize fighting, I'd read the *Police Gazette* enough to know who they were, and they were the best.

"You could learn me," I said. "All I ever knew about fighting I picked up by working at it."

"I'll rustle up some mitts," Eddie said.

There was no sign of Tom Gatty in Milestown— or, as they were calling it now, Miles City— although I covered the whole of it. Most of the time I listened, and what I heard didn't make me feel any better. Yet it was less what I heard than what I didn't hear. There were a lot of suddenly suspicious folks around town, and a lot that wasn't being said.

A stranger coming to Miles City would see just the dusty main street with a row of false-fronted frame buildings along either side. The signs mostly extended from the buildings to supporting posts on the edge of the boardwalk. There were water barrels here and there along the street, in case of fire. Usually one of the Diamond R bull teams was standing in the street, and there were buckboards or other rigs in from the ranches about.

An eastern man looking along that street would think there wasn't much to it, but he would be wrong. In my time I'd been a sight of places, and I'd call Miles City a big town—big in the outlook of most of the folks who lived there, and big in the country it took in all around.

They had law there, but nobody paid it much mind. I mean, when trouble came nobody thought of going to the law about it; you handled it yourself. If somebody made trouble in the town, usually the marshal would run them in for the night; or, if they packed a gun, he'd take their gun away and tell them to go sleep it off.

Times were changing, and there were new faces around. The big outfits were losing stock and they didn't like it. And that meant they would do something about it when they got to the point where they decided action was called for, and I had a hunch that time had come.

As we were going along the street Eddie said to me, "You ought to get you a place of your own, Pronto. A man'll never get nowhere working for the other fellow."

"Never had money enough," I said. "Most money I ever saved was forty dollars, to buy a saddle."

"Why, you must have spent more'n that in Chicago, the way you tell it."

"I did. On'y that was gamblin' money, and gam-blin' money don't stick to a man. Down by the stockyards I got into this dice game, and I was hitting a few hot licks. I started with less than thirty dollars, and ran it up to more than three hundred. Then the cops came, and somebody hollered 'Bull' and everybody grabbed. Mostly they grabbed my money, and I came up short with on'y sixty bucks, and a fine to pay."

"You sure played in hard luck."

"Never knew any other kind, come to think of it, but I never kicked up any fuss about it. I'm a man does his job, and fights a lick or two come Saturday."

"You got to get you a place of your own. Little outfit down on one of these cricks you been tellin' of."

"Trouble is," I said, "big ranchers run cows on most of those cricks. They take it mighty unkind for anybody to go to nesting on their water."

"You need to save your money, get yourself a front," Eddie insisted.

"What's a front?"

"Clothes, that's what. Get yourself some new boots, keep them polished up, get yourself a new hat. Maybe a suit. You look like money, money will come to you."

"Man I knew once, Eddie, he figured like that. He got himself all that outfit you're speakin' of, and a new horse and saddle along with it. So they hung him."

36

"*Hung* him?"

"Sure. There was stock missin', and everybody began to wonder where this cowpuncher got the money for that outfit. They taken him out and hung him on the bridge, just on general principles."

"Didn't he give 'em any argument?"

"No use. He just looked down at the water and told 'em to for God's sake tie the knot tight, because he couldn't swim."

I found that Granville Stuart, who owned one of the biggest outfits in Montana, was in town. He stopped me on the street and offered me a job, but the joker was that I'd be holed up all winter in a line camp with Powell Landusky . . . they called him Pike, too.

There wasn't a better man on the frontier. He was a cowman, trapper, hunter, woodcutter for the steamboats, and one of the best rough-and-tumble fighters you ever saw. Only he had a mean temper, and was quick to fly off the handle. We'd wind up killing each other.

There were a hundred stories about him. One time he tackled a camp full of Indians with a clubbed rifle. They figured nobody but a crazy man would do that, and afterwards they left him alone. Another time an Indian bullet hit him in the face. He rode for a doctor, but his jaw was broken up and it pained him so much he just reached in and tore out a chunk of jawbone so big it had two teeth in it. Marked him for life. I never did hear whether tearing that piece of jawbone out made the pain any better.

ME AND EDDIE finally went back to Charley Brown's and hit that stewpot again. We got there early and Charley looked over at us and said, "You broke again, Pronto?"

"You ever seen me when I wasn't?"

"You always paid up." Charley put his hands on the bar. "Pronto, do you need some cash? I can let you have some."

"We can sleep over to the livery," I said, "an' eat here until you throw us out. Soon as we find a job, we'll ride out."

He stood there quiet for a minute, and then he said, "Pronto, I'm going to put you onto something you may not thank me for. Bill Justin needs two men for his line camp on the Hanging Woman."

"What's wrong with that?"

He just looked at me, and didn't answer. Only after a minute or so had passed he said, "You boys step up to the bar."

We were alone in the place, but I guess he didn't want to talk too loud. He filled a couple of cups with coffee and shoved them toward us.

He leaned his forearms on the bar. "Pronto, this here country is walking wide open into trouble, and you'd be a fool not to see it. And that trouble may bust loose right on the Hanging Woman . . . that's why that job's open."

Well, I looked around at Eddie. "What do you say, boy? It's going to be a cold winter, and a man doesn't have to hunt far for wood up there."

"I been in trouble most of my life," Eddie said, "on'y this time I'd not be alone."

"Charley, you tell Bill Justin he's caught himself a couple of live ones. We'll go."

We finished our coffee and started for the door.

Just then it opened up wide, and a man filled the open space with his shoulders. It was Butch Hogan. Hogan was a bull-whacker for the Diamond R freight outfit, and a fighter from who-flung-the-chunk.

"Howdy, there!" he said, grinning. "If it ain't the little man who likes to fight!"

Now I'm no little man, being five-ten and weighing an easy one-seventy; but alongside his two hundred and forty pounds and his six feet four inches, I might be considered small.

The room was filling up, and I could see they'd been egging him on, anxious for a fight. Well, I hadn't had no fun since the night they pitched me out of that honky-tonk back in Chicago, and maybe tomorrow I'd be headed for the breaks along Hanging Woman Creek.

"Butch," I said, "how tall are you?"

"Six feet four in my socks," he said.

"I didn't know they piled it that high," I said, and hit him.

CHAPTER 4

WHEN MY EYES opened, the sun struck right into them, but it was that spring wagon jouncing over rocks and rough road that woke me up.

It took me a minute or two to realize where I was, and when I did, I didn't like it. There I was, lying on my back on the floor of a wagon with boxes and sacks all around me, and my head felt like it had been kicked by a mule.

There's nothing like lying on the bottom of a wagon whilst the horses are trotting downhill over a rough slope to shake a man up, but when I started to rise I wished I'd had another idea. A shot of pain took me in the side, and when I grabbed my hand to it I fell back on the wagon-bed.

Eddie was settin' up on the driver's seat and he looked around at me. "Well, he didn't kill you, anyway."

"Who? Who didn't kill me?"

"That Hogan, from the Diamond R. He sure enough did a fair country job of dressin' you down, boy. You're lucky to be alive."

"I do anything to him?"

"Whatever you done was a mistake. You knocked him down, and up to that time he'd only been funnin'. After that he set out to take you apart."

Eddie drew up the team in the shade of a cotton-wood. "I was about to wake you up," he said. "I don't know this here country, an' maybe I'm lost. That Mr. Justin, he just pointed me this way and said to follow the wheel tracks until you woke up."

There was a canteen in the wagon and I sloshed some water around in my mouth, then dumped some over my head and the back of my neck. The water was still cold, for it was early morning, and it felt good.

"I'll say one thing," Eddie commented. "For a man who does everything wrong, you ain't bad. You troubled him. A time or two there, I'd say you troubled him."

Looking around to see where we were, I said to him, "You must've started before daylight."

"Yes, *suh!* I surely did. That Mr. Justin he came to me in the livery where we were sleepin' and he said he wanted me to take you to the edge of town. The wagon would be waitin' there . . . and he didn't want anybody to know where you was goin'."

That didn't sound like Bill Justin, but a lot of things had happened since I'd been away.

"Eddie," I said, "you make us up a batch of coffee. I got to study this out."

He started digging around in the wagon, hunting for coffee and a pot, but all of a sudden he pulled up short and stood quiet. Then he said, "Pronto, you come see this here."

41

What he was showing me were two brand-new Winchester 73's, and boxes with about five hundred rounds of ammunition. Alongside the rifles lay two .44-calibre Colts, both new. And with them was a note, scrawled on a paper greasy with gun oil.

I been missing stock.

That was all, with just his initials signed to it, but, with all the guns, and coming from a sober man like Bill Justin, it seemed he must figure he was sending us into the middle of something.

"You want to quit?" I said.

Eddie chuckled. "Where we goin' to go? Mighty soon there'll be snow fallin', and I never did like riding the grub line in snow country."

We drank up our coffee and Eddie smoked a cigarette, and I dug around in my pocket for the butt end of that cigar. When I found it, it was all mashed to nothing. But no use to throw it away, so I put the tobacco in my mouth and chewed it, although I'd never been a hand to chew.

From what Charley Brown had said in his saloon, and now Bill Justin, they must believe that the Hanging Woman country was where the trouble lay, or some of it.

Everybody knew Bill Justin's stock. He had good stuff—mighty few longhorns, mostly short-horn stock brought over the trail from Oregon, and bred up with a couple of bulls brought back from the East. Justin was a shrewd man, and he

42

took account of range conditions. He grazed less stock than most, but on account of that it carried more beef, and better beef. He got premium prices wherever he sold.

Now, such stock was hard to hide, and harder to ship. If he was missing stock, somebody was playing a mighty tight game.

While we rolled along what passed for a trail —just two faintly marked wheel tracks—I puttered around, cleaning the grease from the rifles and loading them up. Then I did the same with the pistols. Come dark, we pulled off the road under some trees where there was a little branch that trickled down toward the Tongue River.

"No fire," I said, as Eddie started to gathering sticks. "Cold camp."

We split a can of beans and a loaf of bread, and afterwards we had a can of peaches. They tasted almighty good.

Where we'd stopped there was a small patch of grass among the scattered trees, and we picketed our horses, then moved back under the trees and rolled out our beds.

If anybody was hunting us, they could follow those wagon tracks with no trouble. Only they weren't close behind us, or I'd have seen them. So if they didn't know exactly where we stopped, they might overlook us.

There'd been no chance to sight in that rifle, but I put it down beside me. I didn't know whether

I could hit anything with the six-shooter or not. Most of the hands I knew packed one around, and if they didn't wear it on their belt they had one tucked away in their bedroll. Me, I'd never even owned one. Even cheap as they were, if a body wanted to buy one secondhand, they were too expensive for me. Usually I'd owned a Winchester, but that was a meat gun, and a man never knew when he might have to brush off a bunch of scalp-hunting Sioux. Though that sort of thing had about come to an end, everybody was wary.

Once I was stretched out under the trees, I started trying to figure out what Bill Justin had in mind. It seemed to me he was hoping we'd get to the line camp of the Hanging Woman without anybody knowing we were there, and he wanted us fixed for a fight when they did find out.

If the rustlers were that bad, Eddie and me could look for trouble. Real trouble.

Time enough to cross that creek when we came to it, so I stretched my muscles a mite, and then sort of let myself relax whilst looking at the stars through the leaves.

Those earlier remarks of Eddie's were beginning to nag at me. Come to think of it, I didn't amount to much. Top hand in anybody's outfit, but what did that mean? Forty a month if I was lucky, thirty if I wasn't, and ridin' the grub line a third of the time, seemed like. And when I got to be an old man, swamping somebody's saloon, or wranglin' saddle stock around a ranch, or rustlin' wood for the cook. It didn't give a man a lot to look forward to.

Somewhere along there I dropped off, and it was coming on toward morning when my eyes flipped open. Just like that, and I was wide awake, and my hand on the action of that Winchester.

"That there's a wagon track," I heard somebody whisper, "sure as shootin'."

"Hell," another voice said, "old Justin's been over this here trail a half a dozen times with a wagon."

"This here track's fresh!"

"I got to see it."

"You think I'm crazy? I'd have to light a match, and if it is that damn fool Pike, he'd be likely to blow my head off. He never did have no more brains than a cougar."

Me, I half raised the Winchester. I'd a mind to dust 'em a mite to teach them their manners.

"They don't call him Pronto for nothin'."

There was a moment of quiet, then the second voice said, disgusted-like, "Aw, come on! You goin' to crawl around there all night? So there's wagon tracks! I can show you wagon tracks in this country been there twenty years!"

There was a creak of leather, then the sound of horses moving off through the grass. I lay back and picked out the one bright star that seemed left and tried to remember where I'd heard those voices before.

After a while I heard a faint stir from where Eddie lay, and thinks I, he's been awake, too. He was layin' for them. It gave a man a good feeling to know he wasn't alone out there. Just the same, as I stretched out to collect interest on a night's sleep, I couldn't help but wonder what all I'd gotten myself into.

Only I couldn't see any other way. Winter was coming on and I had no money, nor any place I could call home. When snow started to fall that line shack was going to look almighty good. It was loaded up with grub, and all we had to do was sit tight and keep an eye on that stock.

But it kept bothering my mind. What would those two have done if they had found us?

And we still had more nights to go before we got to that line camp.

The truth was that I didn't know this country very well myself. I'd punched cows on the Milk and the Musselshell, and one spring I'd worked a roundup over on the Little Missouri, but I'd crossed this part of the country only a time or two, stopping over at Bill Justin's line camp on the Hanging Woman a couple of times.

A long time back I'd helped trail a herd of steers clean from the Brazos down in Texas to the Boxelder Ranch near Ekalaka, which took me to this neck of the woods, so I did know a mite about the country, without laying myself out to be an expert.

Another time I'd stopped over at the line camp when we were riding back from the Hole-in-the-Wall, down in Wyoming.

That was the year I was nineteen, and I was full of ginger. They needed a posse to run down some outlaws who'd stolen horses, so I joined up and we gave them a run for their money right up to the opening in that big red wall. Then we fetched up short.

A man with a good rifle could lie up in those rocks and raise hob with anybody trying to ride through the Hole.

Well, we just backed up and decided we weren't going to catch any horse thieves, so we turned around and rode back up country and went into camp on Clear Creek. The outfit broke up there.

THE LINE CAMP stood on a low bench just back of Hanging Woman Creek, setting in nice among the trees. There was a log cabin with two windows and a door, with a corral close by, and from the door of the cabin a man could see the ford a short distance off, where folks usually crossed the creek.

When me and Eddie drove up, Bud Oliver was standing in the doorway, and he had him a saddled horse right there.

"You taken your time," he said irritably. Then he gave a look around and gathered up his reins. "She's all yourn," he said, and stepped into the leather.

"You ain't going to drive the wagon back?" I asked.

"Hell, no. You tell Justin if he wants that wagon he can drive it himself. I want to get shut of this country, and that wagon's too slow."

Now Bud was a long, lean drink of water with a hawk face on him, and he was stubborn as a hammer-headed bronc, but I had never known him to be so downright skittish before.

"You look like your tail was afire," I said. "What's the trouble?"

"I'm leavin' out of here," he said, "and if I was you, I would too. This is the least healthy country I know of." And he dusted out of there.

Eddie, he taken holt of a sack of spuds. "You fixin' to stay?" he asked.

"Hell, that's what I come for," I said. Then I said, "Eddie, if you want to leave I'll not hold it against you. Me, I never did have no brains when it came to trouble."

So we unloaded the wagon and moved in. By the time I'd unharnessed and turned the team into the corral I'd done some thinking.

Bud Oliver was a good hand, and a nervy man. I'd known him too long to think he'd scare easy, and I thought that if he was so all-fired anxious to ride out of here there was real trouble making up, and not just talk.

This was wild country. It was also wild horse country, and until just a few years ago it had been the heart of the Indian country. Across the river and not many miles off was where General Crook fought the Sioux in the Battle of the Rosebud. It was only fifty or sixty miles to where Custer was wiped out. Not many white men had moved into this country.

There was good grass and there was plenty of water, and most years it was as fine a place to graze stock as a man could want. Cattle fattened on this grass, filled out like grain-fed stock, and if Bill Justin could stick it out he could be a rich man.

The cabin was all swept up and clean as a man could wish. There was an iron cooking range, a mess of pots and kettles, bunks for six men, some benches, a couple of chairs, and a table. A few books and some old magazines were lying around, and everything looked snug and ready for a hard winter.

There was even a stack of logs near the corral, and a lot of cut firewood in the lean-to behind the cabin.

One thing I didn't like the look of. Somebody had worked loose an upright split log in the back of the lean-to so it was a place that could be used to go or come from the cabin.

On a sudden hunch I went out the front door and, turning around, studied the door jamb and the heavy door itself.

Eddie watched me for a moment and then he said, "Something out of kilter, Pronto?"

Me, I slipped out my belt knife and dug into the logs near the door. Took me a minute or two, but when I'd dug around enough I forked out a chunk of lead.

Hefting it in my hand, I noticed four or five more holes in the logs, and I showed Eddie the bullet in my hand.

Somebody had been shooting at that door with a mighty big gun.

CHAPTER 5

EDDIE WENT OVER to the stove and lifted the lid. After a glance inside, he picked up a handful of chips and twigs from the woodbox and started to kindle a fire.

"You want to look around," he said, "hop to it. I'll make out to cook."

There was some saddle stock in the corral, and I taken my rope and walked out there. One was a line-back dun, a quick-moving horse I liked the looks of, so I crawled through the fence and dabbed a loop on him.

When I'd saddled up I led him to the door. "Hand me out one of those Winchesters," I said to Eddie, and stepped into the saddle.

The horse crow-hopped a couple of times to give me confidence, and then of a sudden he really doubled up and went to bucking. He did a fair country job of it, too. I was no contest hand, so I rode him straight up and to a finish, and when he had it out of his system we understood each other.

Eddie had come to the door and watched me. "You can ride," he said, "but that horse didn't mean it. He was just dustin' you off."

He handed me up the rifle and I turned the line-back and went into the trees.

Knowing what might be expected of me, I didn't do it. Instead of dropping down to the river crossing to see who had been using it, and how many, I circled back of the cabin and went up the ridge under cover of the trees.

On this side of the ridge the run-off water ran into creeks and then down to the Hanging Woman. On the other side the water ran down to the Tongue River. At this point it was maybe eight miles between the two, and it was rough country.

At the top of the ridge I looked back across the Hanging Woman toward Poker Jim Butte and the Otter Creek country. You never saw anything more peaceful than that spread of land right then, but I was not a trusting man.

Most of the ridges and buttes were timbered, and there was a good bit of heavier timber along the creeks, with here and there a patch of willows. Drifting down the ridge, I cut back and forth for sign . . . lots of deer, and several bunches of cattle. I startled a couple of elk feeding at the head of Dead Man Creek, but not wanting to advertise myself, I let them go.

A time or two I came on horse tracks. One set was two riders traveling together, cutting across country toward the west. A bit later, just after coming on a set of buffalo tracks, maybe six or eight in the bunch, I found the tracks of another horse.

The hoofprint was light and small, but poorly defined, and that very fact bothered me. Somehow all my instincts told me that hoofprint should be sharply defined. Turning aside, I trailed the prints for a couple of miles until the shadows were growing and it was time to head for the line camp. But before I swung off I had learned a few things.

The rider of that horse had waited for some time in a small clearing at the head of a gulch over-looking the river's ford that was near our cabin. From that spot the rider could watch both the ford itself and the trail approaching the cabin.

There were a good many tracks—the tracks of a standing horse that was impatient to be moving. Although the rider had waited for some time, he had not dismounted, so I had learned nothing of him. Only, judging by the hoofprints the rider could not be a very big man.

When I rode up to the cabin, Eddie stepped out with a rifle in the hollow of his arm.

"See anybody?" he asked.

"Tracks."

I told him about them, and as I was speaking I suddenly knew why those hoofprints had been so poorly defined. That horse wore leather shoes, like those an Indian sometimes uses on his horse. They are fitted snugly around the hoofs, often cut from green hide so they will shrink tight over the hoof, and they are tied or laced there.

Well, the last thing I wanted around here was Indians. The battles of Little Big Horn and Rosebud were nine years past, but there were still young bucks around hunting trouble, and I'd had my share of Indian fighting as a boy.

I went on talking to Eddie. "The grass is good," I told him, "and what I figure we'd best do is wide-circle and push whatever stock we can in toward us. All we can do is sort of start them moving this way. It will save us a lot of riding later if snow starts to fall."

Well, sir, Eddie had fixed us a bait of grub that I never tasted the like of. That man could really cook. Me, I had been throwing stuff together for so long, eating baking powder biscuits, beef, beans, and bacon, that I didn't know what real grub tasted like. When I pushed back from the table I broke a piece of straw off the broom and used it for a toothpick.

I looked up at Eddie. "You're wastin' your time," I said. "Why, cookin' like that, any outfit in the country would hire you on at twice the money. In this country, if you want to keep good hands, the best way is with good cookin'."

I walked over toward the door, which was

53

standing open, and looked out. I didn't walk right up to that door and stand in it—I looked out from well back in the room. But I could see the ford, and three riders were crossing the river, coming toward us.

It was after sundown, and I couldn't make them out, but I could see the water where it rippled around their horses' legs as they splashed through.

"Comp'ny," I said. "You take that Winchester and stand back there beside the window. If it comes to shootin', you take whoever's on the left."

Me, I taken a Winchester and stepped out with it held loose in the hollow of my arm. Like I said, I was never any hand with a short gun, but with a Winchester I could dust things around, and I'd practiced by the hour getting a rifle into action every which way. I could throw one from the hollow of my arm into shooting position mighty fast—or, the way I preferred it, the rifle hanging from a sling, the butt level with the top of my shoulder.

So I stepped out front and waited, watching them come up the slope to the cabin.

Right away I knew these were no punchers riding the grub line. Their horses were better than any remuda would be likely to have—maybe one puncher would have such a horse, but not three in a bunch. I said as much, speaking over my shoulder to Eddie. Three men riding horses like that . . . if they weren't ranchers owning cattle—

unlikely away out here—they were likely to be a posse hunting outlaws, or the outlaws themselves, and Eddie knew where I was putting my money.

When they saw the rifle they pulled up some fifty feet off, and I said, "You boys huntin' somebody?"

"You alone?" one of them asked.

"No, I ain't alone. I got me a Winchester."

"What's the matter? You expectin' trouble?"

"Mister," I said, "I was born to trouble. I never did know anything else, so I'm spooky. Why, I'm so spooky that if anybody was to come prowlin' around I'd be apt to start shootin' without even askin' questions."

"We're huntin' Rafter 88 stock."

When a man has been punching cows since he was knee-high to a short pony, he doesn't have to draw pictures. A Rafter 88 would cover a Bar J like a blanket, and it was a copper-riveted cinch that whoever invented that brand had that in mind.

"Mister, I ain't seen any Rafter 88 stock, but if I do I'll shoot it and look at the hide from the reverse side."

They were sitting back in the shadow thrown by the trees, and I wished I could see their faces better. Nobody seemed to be paying much mind to the cabin, so it was likely they believed I was alone. If they had been tipped off by somebody in town, that might seem possible, for I'd been lying in the back of the wagon and the informer might have seen only the driver.

"That kind of talk won't get you anywhere." The speaker was a tall man with narrow shoulders, and he carried his gun low on his leg like some of the gunmen were starting to do. "You've got a long winter ahead of you, friend. I'd start figuring on lasting until spring."

"You know," I said confidentially, "that's a good thought. That's a thought should be in all our minds. Why, when I came into town and found they'd lynched Rigney and run Chinnick out of town, I decided folks around Miles City were changing."

Right then I lied in my teeth, but I had a hunch that I wasn't far off the track. "Especially after I heard Granville Stuart talkin' to X. Beidler."

Now, Stuart being one of the wealthiest ranchers in Montana, and Beidler being a lawman who had been one of the vigilantes who cleaned up Virginia City, I figured those names would carry weight, and they did.

"What did you hear?"

"Well—nothing, when it comes to that. On'y they were talking mighty confidential, and Stuart wanted to hire Pike Landusky for some kind of a job. And after what had happened in Miles City, I just had an idea they were settin' up a new vigilante outfit to go after stock thieves."

I knew no such thing, but it would do no harm to worry this outfit a little.

"I think he's lyin', Chin." The rider who spoke

was a stocky, barrel-chested man. "This here's Barney Pike, and he thinks he can fight. Let me have him."

"Lay off, Shorty," Chin said. I could see him gather his reins a mite. "We'll ride on." He looked over at me. "Pike, you stay close to that shack this fall and winter, and you might find yourself with a nice road stake come spring."

"I don't need it. I can always ride the grub line."

They turned their horses and rode away, only as they went off Shorty turned in his saddle and said, "One of these days."

And I said, "Any time you want your eyes dotted, you come to me."

Backing into the house, I closed the door. "Stay shy of the windows," I told Eddie. "They might come back."

"What we need," Eddie said, "is a dog. A good dog is a mighty fine thing around a place."

I was thinking about those three men.

Chin Baker was an outlaw from down in the Cherokee Nation. The last I heard of him, he'd killed a deputy marshal in the Cross Timbers and was supposed to have lit out for Colorado and the mines. He was said to be a handy man with a six-shooter.

Shorty Cones was a tough cowhand who had a reputation as a trouble-maker. It was said he was hell on wheels in a rough-and-tumble. He sure seemed to be scratching dirt for trouble now.

The third man hadn't said a word, but I'd noticed that he was a big man . . . mighty big.

"What did you mean about those brands?" Eddie asked presently. "I never had no truck with branding."

"Ours is the Bar J. Well, in the course of branding a lot of stock you slap those brands on fast, and mighty few of them are set straight. In the Justin brand, the bar is over the J, but supposin' a man takes a running iron and adds another bar to the end of the one already burned on? He would rarely find that bar just straight and perfect, so he would slant his bar down a mite and make the bars into a rafter . . . you know, like a peaked roof.

"Then he would finish the curve on the J, bending it around into a loop, and then into another loop to make an 8. Then all he has to do is add another 8 and that steer is wearing a Rafter 88 brand."

"What was that about skinning?"

"When you skin a steer and look at a hide from the back, you can tell if the brand has been worked. That's why cow thieves usually try to get rid of the hides if they do any butchering."

When the shutters were closed and we were tight in our own cabin, I sat by the stove, for there was chill in the evening air, and studied about the situation. The more I studied, the less I liked it. Aside from Indians, I'd done mighty little shooting at folks, and didn't really care to do any.

As far as that goes, Indians and me usually hit it off all right. There'd been war parties a time or two, or young bucks hunting a reputation, or trying to steal horses.

This here was different. It looked like I'd sure enough bought myself a ticket into a shooting war, and worst of all, I'd brought Eddie Holt along with me.

I kept thinking back to Tom Gatty. Was he mixed up in this? I didn't want him to be . . . he'd been my friend, was still my friend so far as that went, and right now I owed him money.

Those bullet holes in the door meant somebody had been trying to run Bud Oliver out of here. Would they try that on me? That was a question I needn't ask. If they would try it on Oliver, who was a good hand, they would try it on me. And I was too damned stubborn to run.

Something told me I should pick up and light out, get out of whatever I was in, but something else went against it. I'd never learned to run from trouble. I just bowed my back and went in swinging with both hands.

Well, there was work to do if I was going to stay—and I knew I was. If we didn't want to be riding all over southeastern Montana, we'd best be bunching some of those Justin cows. There was plenty of feed, unless it was a late spring.

Those stolen cattle . . . to get them to market they'd have to be driven to the railroad, or driven down country. The chances were they were bunching them somewhere in the wild country, holding them for a big drive. It surely wouldn't pay to make a lot of small drives for a long distance.

A man who picked his country could take a big herd quite a ways east without being seen by anybody. There were places he would have to be careful, of course, and he would need some good hands and some organization. If he shipped east, he wouldn't dare hold the cattle long near the railroad—he'd have to drive them in, load up, and ship out.

Of course, a man could sell cattle at Deadwood and in the mining camps, but that was a small operation, handled by ranchers closer to the Black Hills, or in them. All in all, I had a fair idea that the stolen cattle were being driven to the railroad.

When I finally dropped off to sleep that night I was thinking of what Eddie had said: that I should ought to have a place of my own.

Maybe . . . maybe someday.

If I got out of this alive.

CHAPTER 6

WHEN I CAME out of the cabin in the freshness of daybreak it was right nippy. It was early for frost, but you could feel the coming of it in the air. Made a man feel glad he'd a snug place to hole up in, with winter coming on and all.

One thing I could say for Justin. He didn't stint any on the grub. We had cases of tomatoes and peaches in cans, a sack of sugar, plenty of flour, beans, dried fruit, rice, and some big cans of Arbuckle.

When I'd rustled a fire I said to Eddie, "We can take turns cookin' if you're of a mind to, but after you taste mine you may feel you'd like to take over. I was never no hand to cook."

"I don't care if I do, on'y I want to punch cows and I'll never learn how in this here cabin."

"You any good at makin' bear sign?"

"Never heard of it."

"Bear sign is doughnuts . . . sinkers . . . crullers—whatever you're of a mind to call them."

"Man, I make the best doughnuts you ever ate."

So, if I got shot, at least I would die happy.

But I wasn't harboring any illusions. Nothing in life had given me cause for hopefulness. A man went ahead doing the best he could, but it always seemed there was more trouble lurking just around the bend of the road. I had seen some folks to whom nothing ever happened, but that wasn't the way it was with me.

One time I was telling some eastern folks about life on the range. The man of the house, he was a fat, comfortable man eating three big meals a day, he had a fine house and family, and he said to me that he wished he could live my adventurous life. Me, I just looked at him.

61

He should crawl out of bed on a chilly morning on a cattle drive, stagger half blind to the chuck wagon and gulp scalding coffee that would take the paint off a wall, and then saddle up a mean-minded bronc. Then he should get out with a stiff rope and try to do some roping. He should go tearing off down a hillside on a fast-moving cutting horse, and suddenly find a ditch ahead of him that's maybe twenty feet wide and just as deep. . . .

He should work himself half dead with tiredness, and come dragging up to the mess wagon long after dark, eat food that he wouldn't feed his dog, and then roll up in that same cold bed.

Eddie I could understand. He was a colored man and he would get a better shake out west than almost anywhere. He might find some folks a bit stand-offish . . . some people believe because a man looks different that he feels different; but out on the range a man is judged by how he does his job and stands up to trouble.

Me, I wasn't going to do him no favors. If he did his job, well and good. I couldn't care what color he was, or even if he had two heads—so long as both of them didn't eat. I'd already seen him shape up on that trip across country, and I liked the way he did things. He was a stand-up man with pride and strength.

That first day we rode out and around, getting acquainted with the country, moving a little stock. For most of that work we'd be riding out twenty miles or better, but now we were just getting the lay of the land. As we rode I talked to Eddie, telling him what being a cowhand was like.

"Winter is the time when a cowhand—if he isn't out of a job and riding the grub line—is supposed to catch up on his sleep. I never got that lucky. Seems to me I always fall into jobs where I work harder than ever.

"Now, Justin put us out here to bring his stock through the winter, as much of it as we can. Mainly, we'll have to keep holes open in the ice so the cattle can drink. A small hole is best, and make it long. You scatter leaves and truck on the ice so the cattle won't slip and slide too much."

Eddie was listening as I went on talking.

"The grass around here is mostly blue grama —and there's nothing any better—mixed with buffalo grass. It'll stand a lot of grazing, and it re-seeds itself. If the stock can get to the grass, it will do all right, even in winter.

"First, we'll start swinging wide and moving the stock closer to home. There's feed enough and we won't have to ride so far. Pay attention to weak stuff first.

"But most of all, you never stop looking. You look for cattle in trouble, you look for Indians, and you'll look for rustlers. You'll look for any-thing different or out of the way—for strange tracks, or any movement of cattle in a bunch and on a straight line.

"Left to themselves no cow crittur will walk far in a straight line . . . they graze around here and yonder, or they lie down and chew their cud. If they move in a straight line for long, it means somebody is driving them. Going to water is an exception, sometimes, but you'll soon learn to judge."

All the time I talked I was busy looking. There was a big old grizzly in this country, I could tell . . . I'd seen his claw marks high up on scratch trees where he'd made his mark. Grizzlies do that to stake a claim to a piece of territory. If any other bears want to come in, they look at those scratch marks, and if they're too high on the tree they turn around and heist out of there—if they're smart.

I saw wolf tracks, too—tracks of a big lobo that I'd guess would weigh a hundred and fifty pounds . . . and few get that big. There was lots of deer, elk, and antelope too.

We rode up the Hanging Woman to Trail Creek, and then turned east toward the Otter. We found the trail of a travois . . . the two trailing poles on which Indians load their gear to drag it behind a horse or a dog . . . and a small party of Indians—two men and several squaws and youngsters. They were riding west toward the Big Horns. One of the horse tracks looked like something I'd seen before, but I couldn't place it.

It was long after dark when we got back to the cabin, and we came up on it mighty slow and careful, but everything was as we'd left it. After I'd fed the stock in the corrals, I scouted around a bit.

Not that I was looking for anything special. I just wanted to get the feel of the place after nightfall. Everything has a way of looking different at night, so I walked around sizing up the layout from all angles, studying the outlines of things against the sky, testing the night smells.

Something about those smells worried me. There was the smell of the pines, of the creek down below, of the horses in the corral, of smoke from the house, of fresh-cut wood . . . but there was another faint, hardly noticeable smell. Whatever it was brought a feeling of loneliness almost of homesickness, and that I couldn't figure. I'd had no home in so many years that I—

Eddie stuck his head out of the door. "Come and get it," he said, "before I throw it away."

Whatever that smell was, it was like a flower, like some sort of flower had just opened up. And that didn't make sense at this time of year.

FOR THE NEXT five days we had no time to think of anything or anybody. We worked the country west toward the Rosebud, and north as far as the Muddy and Skully Creek, most of the time just starting cattle drifting back to the south and our line camp. It was early for snow, but in Montana a man never could be sure, so we made a quick, scattering sweep across the country to begin, with a view to making a more careful search later if time allowed.

Eddie Holt was a rider, no question about that, and he was a fair hand with a rope, so it took him no time at all to get the hang of it. Of course, knowing cattle comes with experience, and no man is going to get that overnight, but I told him what I could, and the rest he'd have to learn.

The stock was in good shape, although it could stand culling. Some of the young stuff and cows carrying calves we started back toward the Hanging Woman, but we found no tracks that day except the tracks of cattle or wild life.

Along in the late afternoon we pulled up on a ridge near the head of Wolf Creek, and looked down the valley of the Tongue.

"It's a fair land," Eddie said softly, "a fair, wild land."

"It is that," I agreed.

The bright glare was gone, the shadows softening the distance, and the coolness of evening was coming on. Far off an eagle soared against the sky . . . soon he'd be going in, leaving the sky to the owls and the bats. I saw a gray wolf sloping along through the trees, head down, nose reaching out for the scent of game.

We sat motionless and not talking, just taking in the peace of eveningtime. Finally Eddie said, "It was no wonder they fought for it."

"Yeah," I said, "and they *fought,* too. Not many

could beat a Sioux or a Cheyenne when it came right down to fighting."

We turned our horses off the rise and headed back toward home.

"Out here," Eddie said, "a man gets away from it all. I mean, out here he's really free."

"Fewer things to bother," I said, "and fewer folks to bother you with them. But a man can't get away. You can run away, but you can't hide. Things catch up with a man."

Yet what he said worried at my mind. Was that why I was here? Was I running from something? But I'd nothing to run from. I wasn't sore at anybody . . . even when I fought, I fought just for the hell of it, the way some men watch horse races or prize fights, or maybe pitch horseshoes. I just plain liked to fight, with no angry thoughts toward anybody . . . unless a man tried to use me mean. Funny thing . . . I had a whale of a temper, but I couldn't remember when I'd been mad during a fight. They just didn't affect me that way.

Maybe what I was avoiding was the need to try and better myself. That had never seemed so all-fired important. I'd heard a lot of talk about success, but I'd never seen a successful man—what folks called successful—who was happier than me, if as happy.

Eddie had a way of starting me to thinking. Like when he said I should have a place of my own. Well, he was right. I should have such a place.

I had cow savvy. I knew range conditions, and had learned a lot from the men I worked for . . . and some of them could have learned a lot from me.

Bulls, now. A man in the cow business needed good bulls, and they would be finding it out soon. If a man had good bulls he had no cause to worry about his stock. It was time, these days, to start breeding for beef, not to think so much of owning so many head, but of owning good fat stock and good breeding stock. The old days on the range were gone, a man needed less range now, but he needed to care for it, needed to balance his grazing.

But where would I get the money for my own place? Or get the kind of bulls I knew were needed? A man could homestead, but that didn't provide enough range to graze stock. He could homestead a good creek or water hole, and use public range—until folks crowded too close.

It was thoughts like these that were in my mind as we rode back, but a rifle shot broke in upon them.

There's a lonesome sound to a rifle shot in the evening. It sounds, then sort of echoes away, and dies off somewhere against the hills.

We both drew up and sat there, listening to it dying out.

"That was close by," Eddie said.

"They weren't shooting at us, neither," I said.

No answering shot came.

We sat listening for a minute or two, and then

we started down the hills, riding slowly, for we didn't know what might lay before us.

It might have been some Indian hunter killing a deer. I said that, and Eddie agreed, but neither of us believed it. From that moment I think we were sure of what had happened. Somebody, though we didn't know who, had been killed.

And that somebody had been shot from ambush.

Reaching down, I slicked my Winchester from its scabbard; and Eddie, after a moment, did the same. We spread out a little, too, riding carefully down the slope among the trees, ready for what might await us.

During the last few days I'd felt a change taking place within myself. Not that it was unfamiliar, for I'd experienced it once before, a long time ago, and I knew it was something that happens to men—perhaps not to all men—when danger impends.

My whole make-up, all my senses, every part of me was becoming more alert, more watchful . . . and more careful. Where before I might have hurried, might have brushed by a lot of things, now I was listening, I was watching, and every bit of me was wary of danger.

Part of it was the warnings from Justin, from Charley Brown back in Miles City, and from Chin Baker at the line camp. But it was more than that.

What alerted me, what changed me, and well I knew it, was a real feeling of death and danger in the air. I was never the contemplative type. I knew how to ride, rope, and shoot a rifle, and a few other things a man has to know to get along, but of course any man out alone in the world—a rider, a seaman, a fisherman, folks of that sort—any one of them is likely to become thoughtful. And sometimes I've wondered if danger doesn't actually have an almost physical effect on the atmosphere.

I've little to explain such an idea. I'm a man with few words, and most of those picked up in reading whatever came to hand, but it seems to me it is true. There's times when the air seems to fairly prickle with danger. This here was one of those times.

The ridges around were thick with pines, but only a few dotted the long slope toward the bottom of the valley. The descent was gradual, and only a couple of hundred feet in all.

The pines were black now except on the far side where the last of the sun was tipping them with fire. The valley grass was taller, moving a mite in the wind, but everything else was still, and we rode in silence.

We could hear the swish of our horses' hoofs as they moved through the grass, the creak of saddles, and somewhere a night bird called. Every second we looked for a rifle shot, but we heard nothing, saw no one. Only the grass moving in the wind, only the sky darkening overhead.

And then we saw a horse standing, head down,

cropping grass on a flat at the head of Prairie Dog Creek.

The dead man lay close by. The wind ruffled his shirt and touched the edge of his silk handkerchief. There was no need to get down, for I knew him at once. Johnny Ward had been a good hand . . . repping for an outfit from over toward Ekalaka when I'd last seen him.

The bullet had gone in under his left shoulder blade and ripped out the pocket of his shirt. From the angle of the shot and the place it hit, I judged he had been shot from fairly close up.

He had been a nice-looking boy, and he still was, lying there with the dark curls ruffling in the wind. He had folks somewhere back east, I recalled.

CHAPTER 7

WE WEREN'T TALKING much when we got back to the cabin, and we didn't ride up to the door until it was nigh on to noontime.

Nobody in his right mind takes a man's death lightly, and Johnny Ward had been young and full of living. It worried me, seeing him lie like that, but it worried me more when I scouted around, for I found the tracks of that horse with the leather-shod hoofs.

Johnny had been shot in the back whilst walking away from somebody or something, and my guess he was shot at a range of no more than seventy feet or so. Studying out what sign I could find, it was plain enough that Johnny was in no hurry, wherever he figured to go or whatever he was walking away from.

After a lifetime of reading sign a man can see a lot more than appears on the ground, and although I hadn't much to go on, it was my feeling that the last thing Johnny Ward expected was to get shot. He had stopped once as he walked away, maybe to say something or to wave, and then he had walked on four or five steps further.

Whoever had fired that shot had pulled off about as cold-blooded a killing as I ever did see, nailing him with the first carefully aimed shot, and killing him dead.

There was nobody at the cabin when we got back, and no sign that anybody had been there. Neither of us felt much like talking, or even making up a meal. Eddie put together some baking powder biscuits, and we had some baked beans. We made a meal of those, and then I went to the ford and studied to see if anybody had crossed, but there were no tracks.

Standing there beside the Hanging Woman, listening to the water ripple along the banks, I suddenly realized that Eddie and me were fairly up against it. This was no scare. This was the real thing, and we were facing up to trouble, sure enough.

It gave a man something to ponder, realizing of a

sudden that he might go the way Johnny Ward had. There was a good boy, a good rider, and a good hand, and if ever there was an honest man, he was one. And surely that was why he was dead, because he had been honest when somebody wanted him to be otherwise. Or that was how it shaped up.

If it so happened that I was to go like Johnny, there was nobody to mind, nobody that would give it a thought after a few days had passed. It made a man wonder what he had done with his life.

When I went back to the cabin Eddie was reading an old newspaper. He looked up at me. "You think the one who killed that man was the same one who's been shooting at the door?"

"No, there ain't a chance of it. The person who killed Johnny wouldn't have wasted lead. He would've laid out and waited for that one perfect shot, and at fairly close-up range.

"Eddie, we got to face it. We're up against a sure-enough killer. You see anybody riding a horse with leather-shod hoofs, don't you turn your back—no matter who."

He sat quiet for a spell, and then he said, "You going to take the body in?"

"Uh-huh. And I may have to stay for an inquest. Looks to me you're going to be maybe a week or more on your own."

"Don't you worry about me," he said. "You just ride along about your business."

• • •

THERE WERE FOLKS standing along Main Street when I rode in with Johnny. One of the first men I saw was Granville Stuart; another was Bill Justin.

Justin was surprised when I named the dead man. "Johnny Ward? The last I heard of Johnny he was punching cows up on Cherry Creek."

Briefly, I told what I knew, and as I talked several men gathered around, listening. Standing on the walk some distance off, but within earshot, was a man who looked familiar, but I couldn't make out who he was. Stuart asked me a question, and after I answered him I looked around, but the man was gone.

Suddenly it came to me who he looked like. There'd been something about him that made me think of Van Bokkelen, whom I'd last seen back to Dakota.

Next day they had the inquest and I gave my evidence—or as much of it as I felt should be given. In my own mind I was sure whoever rode that leather-shod horse was the guilty party, but to most people that would mean an Indian, and I wasn't about to start an Indian scare.

There'd be loose talk, and then somebody would organize a raid and the Indians would fight back, and we'd have a first-class war on our hands. I was sure in my mind that whoever rode that horse was no Indian, so I kept still and testified to what I had found, adding the fact that Johnny Ward was obviously shot by somebody he knew and had talked with . . . that he was shot down without warning, at fairly close range.

One thing I did say that I was immediately sorry for. They asked me could I identify the track of the killer if I saw it again, and I said I believed I could.

And with those words I stood myself up right in the target rack of a shooting gallery.

There were two or three strangers at the back of the room where the inquest was held, and I didn't get a good look at them. And there was somebody else in the room who was no stranger. Jim Fargo was there.

The place I'd got for myself was across from the livery stable, where they had a few rooms for rent. That night, on a hunch, I shifted the bed as quietly as I could, moving it to the opposite side of the room. No more than a cot it was, and it was no trick to just pick it up and move it. I had pulled off my boots and was getting undressed when I thought of those strangers at the inquest, and it came to me that one of them was Duster Wyman, who'd loaned me ten dollars back in Jimtown— the man who was supposed to be Tom Gatty's representative in the Dakota town.

If I hadn't been so dog-tired I'd have saddled up and lit out for the hills right then.

Like I said, I was never any hand with a six-gun, but since Justin supplied them, I'd been carrying both a six-shooter and a Winchester. When I finally stretched out on the cot I had both of them to hand.

The night noises slowly died away. Boots sounded on the boardwalk, a door down the street slammed, then somebody tripped over a board and swore. At last all was quiet, and I dropped off to sleep.

Suddenly the night exploded with gunfire and I jerked up to a sitting position, six-shooter in hand. Even as I sat up I heard the ugly smash of another bullet that came through the wall, and promptly I fired through the wall in return.

Then there was a moment of stillness, followed by a sudden uproar of voices. In the hall angry questions were called out, followed by a pounding on my door. I swung my feet to the floor and went over and opened up. The proprietor was there, and the night policeman; behind them crowded half a dozen people.

"What happened?" the night policeman asked.

"Somebody shot at me," I said, "an' I jerked up out of a sleep and fired back."

They walked across the room, holding a lamp high. Two bullet holes had come through the thin wall, and if I hadn't moved the bed both of them would have hit me.

"You moved the bed," the proprietor said. "Did you figure on this?"

"Man on the other side of that partition snores," I said, "so I moved over here."

Funny thing was, they believed me. Most of those men knew me and they couldn't figure any good reason for somebody wanting to kill a harmless gent like myself. For that matter, neither could I . . . unless I was getting in somebody's way.

After they left I moved the bed back across the room and went to sleep, but before I dozed off I lay there thinking that maybe this was my time to see California. Somehow I'd always wanted to go there, and they say it can be right pleasant in the winter.

Only thing was, I'd left Eddie Holt out there at the line camp, and he would need help to get through the winter.

The more I thought of it the madder I got, and I'd never been one to back up from trouble. Maybe I would have been better off if I had.

Come daybreak, I went up the street to the Macqueen House and treated myself to a first-rate breakfast, with all the trimmings. It was true I hadn't much cash, but there was enough for that.

I was still sitting there when Bill Justin came in and sat down with me.

"How're things?" he asked.

"You saw Johnny Ward," I answered.

"I mean how're the cattle?"

"Good shape, mostly. I'd say they needed culling. Mr. Justin, you're carrying a lot of dead weight out there. You could round up and ship a good herd of culls."

We talked cow business for a few minutes, and then Granville Stuart came in and walked over to the table. He said good morning to us and sat down.

"Pike," he said, "there are some of us believe it is about time to make a clean-up of eastern Montana—maybe even western Dakota."

Me, I just looked at him, although I was pretty sure I knew what was coming.

"You've got the reputation of being a fighter."

"With my fists, maybe."

"A fighter is a fighter. I want a few good men, Pike, and we've got a few." He named a couple, and when he did I looked at him and shook my head. Granville Stuart was a fine man and a good cattleman, and he was making his mark in Montana; but I'd never put much stock in vigilantes.

"I'm no hand with a gun," I said, "and when it comes to the law, I leave it to the law. If they can't handle it, you'd best get somebody new."

"They aren't equipped to handle it," Stuart said. "It's the same situation as they had at Virginia City."

Well, maybe it was. "No, sir," I said. "I'll stick to punching cows."

"You're right in the middle of the rustlers," Stuart said, showing his irritation. "You've got them all around you out there." He paused. "You've even been shot at."

"Looked like it," I agreed, "and maybe that's

what it was. Well, I'll fight for any stock I'm riding herd on, and I'll do as good a job as I know how, but I'm not a manhunter."

After that they left me. I finished up my meal and ordered more coffee. Compared to what we made at the line camp it was mighty weak stuff, but it was still coffee.

I was paying no attention to anything around me when suddenly a girl spoke to me.

Well, I'd been so taken up with listening to Stuart and Justin that I hadn't noticed that girl before. She had come in after I had and was sitting at the next table. Now I saw that she was a right pretty girl.

"I beg your pardon, sir. Could you tell me how to reach Otter Creek?"

"Where on Otter? That's a long stretch of creek, ma'am." And then I added, "And nothing out there a lady could go to."

"I want to go to Philo Farley's place."

She was slender, and got up mighty stylish, and she had the look of a thoroughbred.

"Are you kin?" I asked.

"Kin?" She looked puzzled, but then her face cleared. "Oh, yes! He is my brother."

Turning around in my chair, I said, carefully as I could, "That ain't much of a place, ma'am. I mean Farley's doing all right . . . or was last I saw him, maybe a year ago, but he built that cabin himself and he wasn't much of a builder.

"He's got him a few cows, and some good horses, and given time he'll make out, but I wouldn't say it was any place for a city woman."

"He needs help." The way she said it was matter-of-fact, no nonsense about it. "If I can help him, I shall." And then she added, "There is no one else."

"Is he expectin' you?"

"No. I knew he would tell me not to come, so I just came anyway."

"I'm going that way, ma'am," I said. "I work for Justin, and he has a line camp out on the Hanging Woman. I can take you out there, but I'd suggest you stay here in town instead, and let me ride over and tell him."

"That's rather silly, isn't it? Why should he make a trip in here for me? If he needs help, that would be time lost, and I am sure time is important to him."

Now, when a woman gets that look on her face there's not much point in arguing with her, but I made one last attempt to get the straight of things. "Did he tell you he was in trouble?"

"No . . . but from the tone of his last letters, I knew he needed help."

She did not have to convince me of that. Philo Farley was a slim young Irishman from the old country, a good man, too. He had been a soldier on the Northwest Frontier of India. He had come to Montana four or five years ago and, after looking around, had picked that site near Otter

Creek and homesteaded it. And he'd had trouble.

There were a couple of ranchers over that way that didn't take favorably to nesters of any kind; and then there'd been a passing war party of young bucks who had decided he was fair game.

The Khyber Pass apparently had taught him a few things, and the Sioux lost a warrior and two horses, with another buck wounded, before they decided to let him alone.

As for the ranchers, they had done nothing, but I knew they weren't taking kindly to his home-steading there, and they had made the usual comments about losing stock. Such comments were occasionally based on fact, but often as not they were just preliminary to some action against the nester. What had followed I had no idea, for I'd been gone from the country for some time.

I left the girl in the restaurant and went out on the walk.

Bill Justin was there, talking to Roman Bohlen.

Bohlen was a big rancher, a rough, hard man, too autocratic for me to work for, although I'd worked beside him on round-up crews. He was a good hand, fed his outfit well, paid top wages, but he was a brusque, short-spoken man whom I never cottoned to. However, he was probably the most successful rancher around, and he carried a lot of weight.

He looked at me, a straight, hard look. "Didn't know you were a ladies' man, Pike," he said. "Who is she?"

Sort of reluctantly, I told him. "She wants to go out to her brother's place."

It wasn't until I'd said it that I remembered Bohlen had been one of the men who had said a lot about Farley. In fact, he had done everything but flatly accuse him of rustling.

"Don't take her out there," he said, and that brusque way of his fired me up. Anyway, he wasn't my boss.

"She asked me, and I'm taking her," I said.

Roman Bohlen's eyes turned mean. "By God, Pike, I told you—"

"I heard you," I interrupted, "and what I do is none of your damned business!"

For a minute there I thought he was going to take a punch at me, but he just shrugged and said, "Take her, and be damned."

As I turned away I heard him say, "If he worked for me, Justin, I'd fire him."

"I'd play hell getting anybody else for that camp, and you damn well know it. Besides, he's a good man."

"Maybe . . . I just wonder why he's so willing to take the job. And he must be kind of thick with Farley to be taking that woman out there."

Whatever was said after that I didn't hear, and didn't want to hear. I was afraid I'd go back and take a punch at Roman Bohlen; and if I did, I'd get licked.

Bohlen was as big as Butch Hogan, but a whole

lot faster. Fact was, he had whipped Hogan a year or so back, and whipped him beautifully. I'd seen it.

Right then it came to me that I'd better get busy with Eddie Holt. If he could show me something about fighting, I'd better have him do it. It was beginning to look as if I'd need it.

When we rode out of town I wasn't thinking about the woman beside me. I was worrying some about what Roman Bohlen had said about Farley. Bohlen was a good hater; and when he made up his mind to believe something, there was no changing him.

Ann Farley drew a deep breath. "Oh, this air!" she exclaimed. "It's no wonder Philo loves it. It's such a beautiful country!"

"Yes, ma'am," I said, but I wasn't thinking about the air or the country just then; I was thinking about Roman Bohlen.

CHAPTER 8

SHE WAS SLIM and tall, and she had the kind of red hair they call auburn—a lot of it. Her eyes were almost violet, and there were a few freckles over her nose.

"You come clear from Ireland?" I asked presently.

"Yes."

"You must think a sight of him."

"He's my brother," she said. Then she added, "Although he's almost like my father, for he always took care of me."

"No other kinfolk?"

"Oh, yes, there's Robert. He is the oldest, but he's never been well. He was thrown from a horse when he was a boy, and he's been crippled since."

We rode on, putting the miles behind us. She sat her horse well, and I was not surprised, for the Irish have many good horsewomen among them, and Philo was a fine hand with any kind of horse flesh, too. He had gentled some bad ones, and I really mean gentled. He was not given to rough-breaking them the way we in Montana did.

She was a lady, every inch of her, I could see that, and there was something clean and fine about her that made a man look twice.

"You took a chance," I said, "speaking to a stranger that way."

She flashed me a quick smile. "But you are not exactly a stranger, Mr. Pike. You were pointed out to me. And when your name was mentioned I remembered my brother had written about you."

"Who pointed me out?"

She hesitated briefly, and then said, "It was Mr. Fargo."

"Jim Fargo?" I was plain astonished.

"He . . . he works . . . worked for a firm our lawyer sometimes employs. When our lawyer discovered I was coming to Miles City, he suggested

I look him up. Mr. Fargo would have taken me himself, but he was busy. He pointed you out, as I've said."

We went on talking, and somehow the miles slipped away quicker than ever before. She got me to talking about myself, and I told her about Eddie, and how we met, and what he had advised, and what I had been thinking about a place of my own.

"It won't be no use, though. I ain't got the cash, and ain't likely to get it."

"But you know cattle. Couldn't you pool your knowledge of cattle and range conditions with someone who has capital?"

"How would a plain cowhand meet somebody like that?" I said.

But then I commenced to think about it. All of a sudden I was getting all sorts of ideas in my head that had never been there before, and each one made me think of others.

It was true that a lot of the biggest outfits in Wyoming were furnished with foreign financing and managed by local cattlemen.

We talked about that, and she began asking questions about the country and where her brother lived and all, and she had a way of hitting on the right question every time, so telling her about it was easy. First thing I knew I was telling her what was wrong with her brother's operation, and the trouble he was in with the big outfits. Most particularly, I told her about Roman Bohlen.

She asked about rustling then, and how it was done, and I explained to her the use of a running iron or a cinch ring, and gave her some examples of how brands were altered, something every cowhand knew.

Whilst I was explaining this to her it came over me how easy it would be to turn Bohlen's RB brand into that Rafter 88 Chin Baker had mentioned. It looked to me as if that brand had been selected with a good deal of care.

When the sun went down I headed into the trees along the Tongue. When we got down, it took me only a few minutes to put up a lean-to for her where she could sleep. Then I put together a fire, for I had a pretty good idea nobody was going to bother a man with a girl along. Not in that country, at that time. You could steal cattle or shoot a man and maybe get away with it, but if you bothered a decent woman you stood a good chance of getting lynched . . . even outlaws had been known to lynch a man for that.

We sat out by the fire talking a long time after we finished eating. Seems there's nothing like a pretty woman to inspire a man to talk a lot about him-self. One thing sure, I decided after I rolled in my blankets, she was learning a whole lot more about me and about Montana than I was learning about Ireland or her.

We were getting close to Farley's place when she spotted the first PF steer. Now, it's second nature for a cowhand to read brands. He rides across country and just naturally notices the brand on every crittur he passes, and without seeming to pay them any mind. He does it without thinking, because he has done it for so long. But this girl, she picked out that first PF very fast, and she was quick enough to make the connection.

"That must be Philo's brand." She hesitated only a moment there, and then added, "And it could be changed into a Rafter 88, too, couldn't it?"

"Yes, ma'am." And then, so she'd know what the situation was, I added more reluctantly, "And so could the RB, Bohlen's brand be changed to Rafter 88."

"Of course." She was thoughtful. "So that is why he suspects Philo."

"Not entirely. A good part of it is because no rancher likes a homesteader . . . a squatter. Whether they kill the rancher's beef or not—and some do—he suspects them of it. What he hates just as much is the grass they use or plow up, and the water they may fence in."

"Is water so important?"

"Uh-huh. There's a-plenty now, because we had a good year, and there've been rains in the Big Horns lately, but in a dry year it can make things mighty mean. Ma'am, you get set for trouble if you figure on staying. Those ranchers don't like your brother a bit."

She looked at me. "You ride for a big ranch, and you don't have anything against him."

"No, I like him. He goes his own way, minds his own business, and he stands up for his rights. But that's all the more reason they don't like him."

I drew rein. "It ain't far now, Miss Farley, and I'd better tell you something. Back there in Miles City they are fixing to set up some vigilantes, and if they do, Roman Bohlen will have his say about them and what they do.

"There's nothing halfway about Bohlen. He'd rather lynch two honest nesters than miss one thief. And anyway, vigilantes have a way of gettin' out of hand. They start out to make the country safe, and then they carry on to settle old scores. You tell Philo he'd better stay close to home. If Bohlen has his say, Philo will be on the list."

"*Philo?* But that's absurd! Philo would never steal anything, least of all a cow. Why, he'd never even have need for such a thing. It's ridiculous!"

"Tell that to Bohlen."

It was only an hour later when we rode up to the house.

Philo came to the door and stood there, shading his eyes at us. He was a sandy-haired man, taller than me, lean and wiry-looking. He had a quick way of walking, a manner a man might think was nervous until you knew him better. Whatever else they might say of him, I don't think Philo Farley had a nerve in his body.

He came a couple of steps toward us as we rode into the yard, looking as if he couldn't believe what he saw.

"Ann?" He spoke her name in a startled, unbelieving tone. *"Ann!"*

She was off the horse and in his arms quicker'n you could say scat, so I swung my horse to leave.

He looked up suddenly, pulling back from her. "Pike, don't ride off that way. Get down and come in."

"Got to get back," I said. "I'm overdue and Eddie will be worried."

"Is that the Negro?"

"You seen him?"

"He was by this way." He gave me an odd look. "I had no idea there were two of you over there."

"I'll be going," I said. Yet I held my horse. "Anything I can do, you just call on me." I said that to her, to Ann Farley. And then I rode away.

But at the edge of the yard I almost drew up. My eyes were on the ground and I saw it plain as could be. Not one track, but a dozen. Swinging my horse to the trough, as if on a sudden notion to water my horse, which I did, I took a careful look about.

There were more tracks at the water trough, some old, some new. And all of them were of those small hoofs wearing leather shoes.

A MOON WAS hanging low and a coyote was singing when I splashed through the ford and came up to the bench above the Hanging Woman. There was no light in the cabin and I drew up, suddenly scared.

"Eddie?" I called it low. "Eddie Holt?"

His voice came out of the darkness near the woodpile, close by but so soft I could hardly believe he was there.

"Man, am I glad to see you!" I could sure hear the relief in his voice. "There's been trouble, trouble enough."

"I'll eat," I said, "and you can tell me."

When I'd stripped the gear from my horse I went into the cabin, where Eddie was laying things out, using a candle hooded by a tomato can.

"I can trip the propper from under it," he explained, "and it snuffs the candle. Mostly I been eating before dark, then laying out until late. I sure enough know why that Oliver had him a back door rigged."

Eddie had baked a mess of beans and pork, and while we ate he told me there had been several shots at the door. They had broken the globe to our coal-oil lamp, and they had almost set the cabin afire.

And then a few nights ago there had been night riders.

"Night riders?"

"Uh-huh . . . wearing sheets like them Kluxers from down south. I guess they figured I'd scare." He chuckled. "I ain't been afraid of ha'nts since I was a boy an' was scared by an owl."

They had come the first night and ridden circles around the cabin, crying eerily into the night. When Eddie grew tired of it, he called out that when their throats got dry they could drink at the creek. At that they'd really got mad, and warned him to leave before I got back, or they'd hang both of us.

That didn't sound like Chin Baker or Shorty Cones. Baker could have gone to shooting right off. It sounded more like some of Bohlen's hands.

For the next few days we worked hard, staying together most of the time, separating only when necessary, and never for long.

Day by day the weather grew colder. Frost came, and the leaves turned red and gold. Overnight it seemed the cottonwoods turned from green to slim golden candles, shimmering in the slightest breeze. There was white frost on the meadows, and the tracks of a horse left a dark line across the meadows until the sun took the frost away.

We drove more cattle in, working dark to dark, up before the sun and no sleep until after the sun was down; and all the time we rode loose in the saddle with our rifles to hand. We saw nobody, strangers or anyone else.

Then, after we'd had a few warm days, we took some time off and sharpened up the scythes and cut hay in the meadows. We put the rack on the wagon, and hauled the hay up to the corral and stacked it. I'd cut hay as a boy, but was no hand like Eddie, who swung that scythe with long, easy strokes and laid the hay in neat swathes.

And then one night there was a skimming of ice in the barrel at the corner of the cabin.

Two or three times when we quit early, Eddie began showing me something about boxing. He had done like he said, and had rustled up some boxing gloves before leaving Miles City—got them from Charley Brown, in fact. There was a flat place under three trees, and we boxed there. We filled a bag with sawdust from where we'd been using the cross-cut saw cutting up logs for the winter.

He started showing me how to punch straight, to jab, and to cross, how to work in a clinch, how to tie the other man up. And he added a few wrestling tricks, no good in a boxing ring but very good in a street fight.

That Eddie was as smooth as you ever saw. He never seemed to hurry or take any pains, yet I couldn't have hit him with a handful of seed corn.

But I took to it right from the start. Fighting was something I had always liked, and Eddie knew how to teach.

"All scientific boxing is," Eddie said, "is just a lot of things men have learned over the years. A straight punch is faster than a swing, because it's the straightest line to what you're aiming at. And you don't punch *at* something, you punch *through* it."

During all that time we had no trouble. Our work was hard, rough, and cold, but we stayed with it. Once in a while we'd take a day off, and sometimes we'd box or practice for an extra hour or so. But all the time I had an uneasy feeling that we were living in a fool's paradise.

There was an itch in me to ride over to Farley's outfit, but I held back. I had sense enough to know why I wanted to go, but sense enough, too, to know that such a girl as Ann Farley would never be interested in a forty-a-month cowhand, even if he spoke decent English, which I didn't.

Nobody had shot at the cabin since I'd got back, nor had we found any of those leather-shoe tracks around.

Everything stayed quiet, until one morning we rode out and found that during the night somebody had made a gather of the cattle we'd been driving in. Sixty or seventy head had been rounded up and driven south.

"We'd better pack some grub," I said to Eddie. "This may take a few days."

"We going after them?"

"You ain't just a-woofin'," I said.

The sun wasn't an hour older when we rode out of there and headed south, following a broad trail up the valley of the Hanging Woman.

CHAPTER 9

RIDING SOUTH ALONG that trail gave me time to do some thinking. The trail was wide enough and plain enough, and it was obvious the rustlers were either not worried about being followed, or else they felt strong enough to take care of themselves. In either case, Eddie and me were likely to find ourselves in all kinds of trouble.

Yet that was not what kept me studying. I was trying to pull together all the loose threads, some of which were plain enough.

The starting point had to be Jim Fargo. If he was a Pinkerton man, that would account for Ann Farley's lawyer knowing about him. He had been hunting Van Bokkelen, but the last we'd seen of Van Bokkelen was back in Dakota—unless that was him I'd glimpsed on the street in Miles City.

That accounted for Fargo, anyway.

And if he was a Pink, he might have been taken off that case and shunted out here to handle the rustling investigation. The Pinks usually only worked on train holdups and the like, but they had worked at times on rustling too.

There in Jimtown I had come across Duster Wyman, and he was working for my old friend Tom Gatty. He had money; and Gatty, according to what I'd heard, had money. And it had come from somewhere.

Thinking back over what I knew of Gatty, I decided it wouldn't surprise me none if he took to rustling, and he would know the best trails out of Montana and Wyoming into the Dakotas.

No thief ever knows when he's well off, and every one of them thinks he is going to be the one who gets away with it. To be a thief at all, a man has to be either a damned fool or mighty egotistical, and it could amount to the same thing.

These fellows had been stealing cattle and they were getting self-confident, and when a man gets over-confident he invites trouble. They always make light of honest men, but what they never seem to realize is that honest men can get mad. And from the way Stuart, Justin, and Bohlen were talking, I surmised the time had come.

But none of my thinking explained the leather-shod horse, although it was a cinch that horse was somehow involved. Of that I was sure.

"Pronto," Eddie asked, "if we find those cattle, what do you figure to do?"

"Ain't decided. Maybe we'll hike back and round up some help; or I may just go bulling in there and bring them out my ownself."

He looked at me, but he didn't say anything.

This was some of the finest grazing land in the world when the season was right. If you had rain, or good winter snows that could melt and sink in, you had grass, and a lot of it. And these rustlers were driving the cattle right up the Hanging Woman. I began to ride a first-rate hunch.

"They're headed for Squaw Butte," I said to Eddie, "and from there they'll drive across to the Bear Lodge Mountains."

"How many do you think there is?"

"I've seen the tracks of four, maybe five riders, and by the time we get to Squaw Butte we won't be more than an hour behind them, probably less. The way I figure it, they'll hustle those steers right along."

We camped under a shoulder of rock on Trail Creek, where there was a small space of hard-packed sand and a trickle of water from a spring. There were no trees, just some low-growing willow and chokecherry, but there was some grass further down the hollow where we staked our horses.

Our coffee we fixed over a fire you could cover with your hand, that let the smoke rise through the willows so it would be dissipated by the branches, how mighty little of it there was.

Bedded down there, I lay with my hands clasped behind my head and stared up at the stars. What worried me most was those tracks I'd seen around Philo Farley's place, the tracks of the man who killed Johnny Ward. And with this worry, Ann Farley's face stayed with me . . . some man was going to be mighty lucky to get her. Thinking about that, I fell asleep.

We cut out before sunup, riding fast toward Squaw Butte. It was in my mind that they would hole up there overnight, and be in no hurry to start out at dawn. They would have reached the Powder River too late to cross last night, and they wouldn't attempt a crossing until full daylight. The Powder wasn't deep, but there was quicksand in some places and cattle could get mired down and have to be hauled out.

An hour later, as the sun was just topping out on the far-off hills, we reached the shadows west of the Squaw Butte. If they were smart they would have had somebody up there on the butte watching their back trail, but by now they must feel pretty sure of themselves. And even if they had some-body up there, I had an idea we'd made it into the deeper shadows before it was light enough to see movement out on the open plain.

We worked our way up the side of the butte, keeping under cover of the pines as much as we could, although in places the cover was sparse. When we topped out on the ridge we were under cover of the trees, and we could see the herd down there below us, a couple of miles off. It was right close to Cabin Creek, and we could look across the herd toward Spotted Horse Creek.

We worked our way south along the crest of the butte, keeping under cover, and presently I saw a trickle of smoke coming up, and then I could see the dust where one of the rustlers was working out one of his rough string. The horse was giving him trouble, but he stayed with him. The man himself I couldn't make out.

Studying the country below, I spotted a draw through which a man might work his way close while still under cover. Pointing it out to Eddie, I led off along the hill.

When we were closer, I took another look. Near as I could make out, there were four riders down there, but I couldn't tell who they might be—and that might make all the difference. There's some men will fight, no matter what; and there's others who simply won't. Neither kind worried me much. It was the in-between ones that bothered me, the ones who might do any fool thing.

We swung around and crossed the river upstream of the herd and cut back into the Powder River breaks to the banks of the Spotted Horse. As I'd guessed, only one rider had crossed with the cattle, the others were behind them, pushing them on. And that one man was Shorty Cones.

He came up out of the willows, trying to keep the cattle bunched, and was within thirty feet of me before he saw me. And when he laid his eyes on me he was looking right into the barrel of a Winchester.

Now, Shorty was a cocky, belligerent man, but he was no damned fool. He drew up quickly and reached for the sky with both hands.

"Eddie," I said, "put a loop over that one, and get his guns."

Like I've said, Eddie was a hand with a rope. He'd learned from the trick ropers on the Buffalo Bill show, and he flipped a noose over Shorty's shoulders, snaked it tight, flipped a loop of the rope over him, and moved in to get his guns. He did a quick, expert frisk for hideout guns, and then we took Shorty off his horse and rolled him into a neat bundle. We stuffed a gag into his mouth and left him there. Then we rode out after the others.

It was simple as a 'coon pickin' persimmons. They just rode out of the Powder and right into our hands.

We disarmed them and tied them up, bunched together, and then I said, "Where you takin' these cows?"

Actually, none of them were cows, but we used the term loosely in those days.

Nobody answered, and I hadn't expected it, really.

"Now, look," I said, "I got nothing against you boys but a long ride and a lot of trouble, none of which pleases me. We've got the rope and we've got the tree, and there's nothing to stop us from stringin' you up.

"In fact," I added, "they're settin' up an order of vigilantes to do just that. If you boys were wise you'd light a shuck for Texas. And I'm going to give you a chance."

None of the lot were known to me but Shorty Cones, although one of the others I'd seen somewhere. They were a low-down outfit, all told, but it wasn't in me to see a man hang without he had a chance. Although Roman Bohlen wouldn't be apt to give them any show at all.

"I'm taking your horses, and your guns, but I'm going to turn you loose. My advice to you boys is to get out of here like you was a bronc with a fire under his tail. You come around again and I won't be so easy on you."

Nobody said a word. Eddie rounded up their horses, and we loosened the knot on one man's ropes. Then we started our cattle back across the river and toward home.

"You may be sorry for that," Eddie commented mildly. "That Cones . . . he don't like you none at all."

"They have their chance."

If they were smart, they'd ride out of the country, and they'd start right away; but knowing something of people's unwillingness to believe, until too late, that anything could happen to them, I doubted if they would go. Nonetheless, I wanted nothing to do with hanging any man.

We kept close check on our back trail, but nobody followed us.

"You're a kindly man, Pronto," Eddie said, "but you can only be kindly up to a point, when you live in a world where evil men go armed."

He was right, of course, and I was realist enough to know it. And I knew myself well enough to know that I'd go along with being kindly just so far, and then I was going to spread my feet and start swinging. Last thing I wanted was trouble, but I'd had it before, a-plenty, and met it.

During the night there was a light fall of snow, but it was gone by noon the next day. There was good grass, and we grazed the stock as we went back.

Two nights later we were sitting in the cabin by the fire. Eddie was reading an old copy of the *Police Gazette*, and I was studying through a beat-up old *History of England* that somebody had left there. It had been there all the while, but I hadn't thought of opening it up until I'd talked with Ann Farley.

I'd scarcely got started reading when there came a call outside. "Halloo, the house!" And after a minute or two, "Pike? Can we talk?"

Eddie reached for his rifle, and I got up, dowsing the lamp. I had known that voice.

I opened the door and called out, "Tom? Tom Gatty?"

"Sure as shootin'!" came the answer. "You old Souwegian, you! It's good to see you!" He came riding up, but walking his horse easy so there wouldn't be any mistake.

"You alone?" he asked. He tried to peer past me into the blackness of the cabin, but I knew he could see nothing. There was a red glow of fire on the hearth, but Eddie was out of sight near the window.

"I owe you ten dollars, Tom," I said. "I'll pay you when I draw down my first pay."

"Aw, forget it! What's ten dollars?" He was riding a fine black horse with a new saddle and bridle. He looked prosperous, all right.

He hooked one leg around the pommel of his saddle and started to build a cigarette. "You were kind of rough on my boys," he said. "You set them afoot."

"They didn't have to walk as far as they made us ride after them."

He threw me a sharp look. "How'd you figure that?"

"Tom, you forget who you're talkin' to. I've known you too long, and right away I pegged it. The way they pushed their stock I knew they'd have to have horses stashed and waiting for them somewhere. Knowing you, I knew where that would be—just where we camped one time a few years back. I recall you made some comment at the time, how hard the place would be to find unless somebody knew about it. You had horses waiting in that notch back of Dead Horse Creek."

He chuckled, but there was no humor in it. He was sore to think I'd remembered that place. Maybe he'd forgotten how he found it with me along.

"Pronto, why don't you two throw in with us? We're going to get rich, believe me."

"You know Roman Bohlen?"

"You wouldn't even have to rustle," he continued. "You could handle one of our camps."

"Roman Bohlen," I said, "is going to sweep this country, and he'll be carryin' extra ropes. If I was you I'd light out, Tom. No, I'll be damned if I throw in with you. You know me. I always rode for the outfit, and I always will."

He was irritated, but I thought he was worried, too, but not about Bohlen. "Pike, there are some of the boys who didn't favor me coming here tonight. They were for burning you out, and either running you off or leaving you dead. If you don't come with us, get out . . . I won't tell you again."

"Tom," I said, trying to keep my voice calm, "you know better than to try scarin' me. I don't scare."

He swung his horse. "The hell with you!"

He started to ride off, then he stopped. "Pronto, who rides a horse with leather-shod hoofs?"

"Whoever rides that horse," I said, "killed Johnny Ward. There will be deputies down here hunting around."

Then he rode away, but it left me thoughtful. Tom Gatty didn't know who rode that horse any more than I did, which meant it was hardly likely the rider was a rustler—at least, not one of his outfit, anyway.

Actually, few rustlers were killers. They stole cattle, and if they killed a man it would be while running off the cattle or during a capture; it would be during a fight, and not by intention.

Ice froze on the creek that night, and with daylight I was out showing Eddie how to chop a proper drinking hole for stock.

CHAPTER 10

THERE FOLLOWED A week of as pleasant a time as any working cowhand is likely to have. On the second day Eddie stayed in and made a washtub full of bear sign, and whenever we went out a-horseback we taken a saddlebag stuffed with those doughnuts.

It was clear, cold, and still most of the time. We kept the holes in the ice open for the cattle, checked the tracks in the snow, and snaked one big old steer out of a brushy bottom where he got himself tangled up. Toward the end of the week, Eddie killed a mountain lion that was stalking a calf. Two days later I rode into a pack of wolves and killed two of them.

Because of the hard work we had done in the weeks before the first snow we had most of the Justin stock in an area not over five miles square. There was shelter from the wind if they wanted to seek it, there was a plenty of feed, and there was water. That same stock had been scattered over thirty miles of country before we went to work.

Nobody came by our way, and we saw no more horse tracks of any kind.

Eddie was as good a hand as a man could wish, and he learned fast and stayed with it.

Had this spell in my life come to me before Eddie put that idea in my mind, I'd have enjoyed it more. Maybe it wasn't Eddie alone, for from time to time, and more often of late, I'd been somehow discontented. Now the idea of going back into town and whipping Butch Hogan didn't seem the way it had. Nor did the thought of just being holed up warm and snug for the winter please me as much as I'd expected. I kept thinking of next spring, when I'd be no further along except for my winter's wages—little enough in cash, when a man came to think of it.

Maybe the realization that Ann Farley was just over the rise in the mountain worried me, too. Supposing I met a girl like that, supposing I wanted to ask her to have me, what could I offer her? Life on a cowhand's wages?

So all the time I rode the range my mind kept worrying with the idea of what to do. From time to time I'd recall what Tom Gatty had said about getting rich, but that idea didn't take any hold in my mind, and I'd no sooner think of it than I'd throw it out and turn to thinking of something else. But how was a cowpoke to get ahead?

Late one afternoon who should come riding in but Tom Gatty again.

"Pronto," he said, "I hadn't figured to come back no-how, and now that I've come, it's to ask a favor."

"Go right ahead and ask. You've favored me a time or two."

"Well," he said, "it ain't good for me in Miles City right now. Folks take notions, like you advised when I was here last. I can't go into town, and I'm fresh out of Vegetable Balsam, and if I don't get some I'm likely to die."

"We've got some Gardner's Horse Liniment," I suggested. "Have you tried that? Good for man or beast."

"I got to have the Balsam. And don't take nothing else, Pronto. Don't let them talk you into no cheap, untried medicines. I don't want nothing but Dr. Godbold's Vegetable Balsam of Life."

"We've got some Dr. Robertson's Stomach Elixir," Eddie commented. "My mama swore by it."

Tom Gatty eyed him suspiciously. "I don't know. That there Balsam is the best I ever did see, and nobody has tried more patent medicines than me. Ain't that right, Pronto?"

"Oh, sure! Back in the bunkhouse, days when we punched cows together, Tom had his own shelf right over his bunk. You never did see such a pile of medicines."

"Hell, Pronto, I'm a sick man! You know that. I've always been ailin' and might have died years ago if it hadn't been for that *Home Medical Adviser* I found in the line cabin that winter. Why, I was coastin' right down the slope into the grave until I learned what all was wrong with me."

"That's right, Eddie." I spoke seriously. "You'd have thought him the picture of health, never had a sick day in his life, eat enough for two men and work as hard as any man—or half as hard, we might say. And then he found that book."

"Deceiving, that's what it is. I could have been dead right now. Thing that saved me was Peter's Pills, that and Dr. Fahnestock's Celebrated Vermifuge. Even so, I like not to made it until spring."

He accepted a cup of coffee. "I tell you nobody ever had more symptoms than me. I used to set up half the night studyin' that there *Adviser*, until I near wore it out. I hadn't nothin' to read but that and a mail-order catalogue, but the catalogue couldn't hold a candle to that *Adviser*. Why, I've heard folks talk of Shakespeare, but for sheer writin' the man who wrote the *Adviser* had it all over him. When he got to describin' a disease he was somethin' fierce! And he had him a list of operations that would curl your hair."

Gatty took a gulp of coffee. "That Shakespeare, now. I think he *borrowed* a lot here and there. Why, ever' once in a while I'd come on things in his plays that I'd heard folks sayin' for years. All he did was write them down.

"And for blood and thunder! Why, he killed more folks in one story than was killed in the Newton massacree, the time those Texicans shot it out with the town marshal and Jim Riley come in at the end and summed it up for 'em with his six-shooter."

Gatty glanced over at the table. "What's that I see? Don't tell me you've got bear sign? Why, I could eat my weight—"

"Think you should?" I interrupted mildly. "You're fresh out of Balsam, and I've heard it said doughnuts are hard to digest."

Tom Gatty's hand hesitated while his will poised above his appetite and lost. The hand descended and came up with a doughnut. "I ain't had one of these in years," he said.

Later, when Gatty had ridden off into the night carrying with him a sack of doughnuts, he was also carrying the bottle of Dr. Robertson's Stomach Elixir, dusty from years of standing on the shelf.

Eddie, he listened to the beat of the horse's hoofs until they died out. "That man tried to steal our cattle," he said.

"It wouldn't have been polite to mention it," I said, "on a social occasion."

However, while Tom was tightening his cinch, I had mentioned it in a way.

"Tom," I said, "we welcome your comp'ny, but if you know any rustlers who might still be thinking of Justin cows, you tell them to stay clean away.

"The first time I taken that as good fun . . . the second time I'll come a-shootin'. I ain't no gun-fighter, an' you know it, but you've seen me lay out a runnin' antelope, and if I have to come again, this here and our previous ride are all the warning we'll give. We'll shoot—like we've been shot at—wherever we see anybody near a Justin cow."

Tom, he just grinned at me . . . and then he belched.

"Sorry," he said, and he added, "About them cows—if I come across any rustlers, my advice will be to lay off." He gave me another grin. "I wouldn't want to cut off the supply of bear sign."

Just before I went inside, I felt something wet and kind of light and cold touch my cheek. I turned my head and saw snowflakes on my shoulder and sleeve.

It was cold when morning came. The inside of that cabin, even with a banked fire, was like ice. Me, I huddled under blankets and a buffalo coat, looking across the room at the fireplace and cussing myself for being the first one awake. I lay there trying to decide how many steps it would take to cross that cold floor, how long to get a fire going, and how many steps back to the warmth of my bunk, where I'd stay until the fire was going good.

No use to lay there and wish that fire going. Long ago I learned nothing gets done just by wishing. You have to do it.

In two long steps I was across the room and grabbed up a small handful of pitch-pine slivers, slim, dark red shavings heavy with pitch. Stirring up a feeble glow among the gray of the ashes, I placed the slivers across coals and huffed and puffed until a blaze sprang up. As the fire reached the pitch and discovered what it had to burn, flames leaped up, then I piled on heavy pieces of bark and dry wood and ducked back into bed.

When I looked across the room, Eddie grinned at me. "I was hoping you'd do that," he said, and I swore at him.

Whilst he worked up some batter for hot-cakes I went outside. It was cold . . . the snow lay six inches deep all over the place, and the air was still filled with heavy, slow-falling flakes.

I forked hay to the horses and prowled around a bit. Any tracks not made within the past hour or so would have been covered, and I saw none. I took up an axe, and I listened to the crunch of my boots in the snow as I walked down to the Hanging Woman. It was frozen over, bank to bank.

I chopped a hole in the ice, and mentally tabbed places for the other holes I would have to open here, and in a couple of creeks nearby. Maybe, even, I should do it in Otter Creek.

No sooner had I thought that than I asked myself whether it was really necessary to do this, or whether it was an excuse to ride by the Farley place. But all the time I knew—necessary or not, I was going to ride over.

The ride would be long and cold, but with a good breakfast under my belt and a lunch packed, along with a sack of Eddie's bear sign as a gift, I started off, riding a big roan gelding that I thought would be a good winter horse.

It was after seven when I rode away from our place, and shy of three in the afternoon, guessing by what sun I could see, when I topped out on the rise above Farley's cabin. Twice I had stopped to chop holes in the ice, once on the South Fork of Lee Creek, and again in Tooley Creek.

The wind had started to rise, swirling the snow in the air. I came up through the pines and paused there, looking for a good way down the mountain to Farley's. And then suddenly I realized that Farley's cabin wasn't there anymore.

For what must have been a couple of minutes I sat my saddle staring down into the basin, unable to believe it. Had I made a mistake in the snow and chosen the wrong valley?

No . . . what remained of the corral was there, although covered with snow. And the cabin was gone, no question about it.

My heart began to pound and my mouth felt dry. Without hesitating any further, I started down the slope.

When I rode into the clearing I could see the snow-covered ruins of the cabin, and when I got down and kicked away the snow I saw that the remains of the logs were charred by fire. A section of the corral fence lay flat on the ground, and I knew what that meant. It had been pulled down by a rope thrown over a post, as I had seen many a nester's fence destroyed.

Right then I was scared . . . I was scared of what I would find next. But when I looked the place over, I found no bodies. Whatever had happened to Philo and Ann Farley, they were not here.

And just then my roan whinnied.

Two riders were coming down the slope opposite to the one down which I had ridden. When they saw me they spread apart a little, and I shucked my Winchester and looked right and left for shelter. There was none. If I started to run for the woods I'd be caught, cold turkey, against the white of the new-fallen snow.

True, the snow that was falling now blurred the air between us, but it wouldn't stop a bullet. So I sat my saddle and waited, letting my horse shift around nervously to keep his muscles loose and ready if we had to run anyway.

Both of the men were known to me. Johnny Ives was a youngster with a reputation as a gunfighter. He was said to have killed a man in Kit Carson, Colorado, and another at Doan's Store on the Texas Trail. The only man I actually knew of him killing was an old Indian up near Glendive.

The man with him was a bad one, known around

as George Woll. Somebody had said that Ives was riding for Roman Bohlen.

"Kind of off your range, ain't you?" Ives said.

"Don't know. My range has always been wherever I wanted to make it."

"Like down around Squaw Butte?"

"What's that mean?"

Ives had the thong off his six-shooter butt but I had my Winchester in my hands. He would never lay a hand to that gun in time, and I think he guessed as much. George Woll sat his saddle, motionless.

"I don't know," Ives said, "only you might have been driving cattle down there."

"I was. I drove some *back*."

"You better be able to prove it," Ives said, grinning unpleasantly. "Bohlen's figuring on asking you."

"Let him ask." Gesturing at the remains of the cabin, I said, "What happened here?"

"Hell, do you need a map? Farley was a goddamn rustler an' nester. He got what was coming to him."

Like I said, I've got a temper, and right then it got away from me. "If you say Philo Farley was a rustler, you're a damned liar!"

Ives' face went white and he started a hand toward his gun, but my rifle muzzle had him dead center in the belly, at no more than fifteen yards. "Go ahead goddamn you!" I said. "Go ahead and lay hand to that gun!"

Oh, he wanted to! He wanted to the worst way. And Woll, he just sat there and looked at me as if his face was frozen from the cold, but he kept his hands in sight and didn't make a move or say a word. I decided that I was going to watch my back when George Woll was around.

I was mad clean through. "Philo Farley," I said, "was a gentleman, and if he has been murdered, I'll lay a bet every damned one of you hangs for it!"

"Hangs?" Ives said startled. "For killin' a nester?"

"If you've killed him, you've killed the wrong nester," I said, more quietly. "Philo Farley was a former officer in the British Army, a man of good family, a man with connections, and if you've killed him you've blown the top off this whole country!"

"Aw, he wasn't that important," Ives scoffed. "And if he was, what difference does it make? This here's a long distance from England!"

"Is it? I can name you five big outfits within two days' ride that are English, and all of them friends of the Farley family."

Right there I was stretching a point, but Ann had said they knew some of the ranchers' families in England, so I might be more right than I could swear.

"What became of her?" I asked then.

"Her?"

"Ann Farley . . . Philo's sister."

Ives shot a quick, scared look at Woll. Then he said, "He didn't have no sister that I ever heard of."

"He had one. She just got here from England. I rode out with her myself."

They were really scared now, and Ives gave an apprehensive look at the snow-covered ruins. "I never saw any woman. Farley was always alone."

Woll spoke for the first time. "You seen him?"

So Farley was not dead. Or if he was, they were not sure of it.

CHAPTER 11

WHATEVER THEIR URGE for trouble when they rode into the valley, it was gone by now. They would need time to figure out whether I was lying about Ann Farley, and also they would want to ask Bohlen about Philo himself.

These were not outlaws. They were cowhands, a bit tougher than average, or perhaps only more callous; and to their way of thinking they had been doing the right thing. They rode for their outfit, and the big outfits all hated nesters, and some nesters stole cattle. At least, they lived off the beef of the big cattlemen—or so it was generally believed.

And to the cattleman's way of thinking, it was

even worse that they squatted on good grassland close to rivers, springs, or water holes. They planted crops, they put up fences. And to the cattlemen water and grass were their very life blood.

It was a war for the land, with the initial odds all on the side of the big outfits, but as time went on the numbers were on the side of the nesters. It was not that they were organized, but simply that they kept coming. They were murdered, starved out, or driven out, or they simply couldn't take the hard work, the cold winters, and the endless struggle to make a living that was necessary to homestead in Montana and the Dakotas, and therefore many of them left. But others came, and continued to come.

Some, like Philo Farley, started small cow ranches of their own, and some—and this was also true in his case—came because they liked the wild, free riding country and the rugged life out at the end of creation. The average cattleman was contemptuous of the nester, but in that he was often wrong. Many of those who came west to homestead were just as tough, just as enduring, and just as able to fight for their rights as any cattleman.

Philo Farley was born to the wild lands, and when he got a taste of it on the Northwest Frontier of India, he knew he could never settle for anything less. I had a feeling that Ann was the same sort . . . or maybe I was just telling myself what I wanted to believe.

Not many of the riders for the big outfits knew

Farley, although he was well known among business people in Miles City and Cheyenne, and he had friends among the backers of the big cattle outfits, and among those ranchers from England who had themselves settled in Wyoming.

Actually, I was one of the few who knew him well. Most of the boys thought him too British and stand-offish, but I knew better. He was a strong, rugged man, a dead shot with any kind of weapon, a fine horseman, and a good stockman. He'd had a lot to learn when he came west, but he learned it fast.

Roman Bohlen, who had the largest outfit of any of Farley's neighbors, simply did not like him. He didn't know him, but to a man of Bohlen's temperament that was not at all necessary. Had he known Farley he would have liked him even less, for Bohlen's bullying nature would have clashed with Farley's.

True, I'd been out of this part of the country a good bit, but I had stopped by his place when riding through, had eaten supper with him several times, and we'd had drinks together in Miles City and Cheyenne. Once we had run into each other in Deadwood, where he had come to see how the mining was done. We rode from there to Cheyenne together.

Woll and Ives had plenty to think about now. It was no small thing to kill a woman, and if they had done that they were in real trouble. They would ride off to think about it now, and probably to see Roman Bohlen.

So what was there for me to do? Sitting my horse as they turned away from me, still holding them under my rifle, I puzzled it over in my mind, anxious to make the right move.

Whatever my move was, I had very little time. If Philo or Ann was wounded or hurt, they could not last long in the cold. It was hovering around ten above zero right now, and would fall to zero with night. A man who has lost blood is in no shape to survive under such conditions.

The snow had covered all tracks and was still coming quietly down, not a thick snow, but steady. It would, within an hour or two, cover my own tracks.

My horse was restless, so I swung a wide circle around the ruined shack and the pulled-down corral. Farley had had some fine horses here, but more than likely they had been driven away to survive as best they could somewhere on Bohlen's range . . . he could always pick them up later. Bohlen was no thief, but horses left behind on the range, or cattle, would be appropriated without any thought about it.

Their bodies weren't in the ruins, that was sure, and the two Bohlen riders seemed to believe Farley had escaped. So his sister probably had, too.

To where?

The nearest place where they might be welcomed was the Justin line shack, where they knew I was. Ann did not know where it was, but she had an idea, as I'd pointed out the way to her. And Philo had ridden by there a time or two in times gone by.

Where else would they have gone? They would need shelter at once, and they might well have escaped while the cabin was under fire . . . or perhaps when it had been left burning. But Woll and Ives evidently believed that Farley was either dead or dying, so they must have hit him. Which could only leave the possibility that Ann had gotten him away. Philo might have been conscious enough to direct her where to go.

There were always places a man could hide if he knew where to go; and in riding around the country, hunting or rounding up strays, a man soon knew every nook and cranny of the hills—or thought he did. So I went through my mind trying to think of a place they might have gone.

It would have to have shelter from the snow, and wood to burn, and be a place Bohlen's men either didn't know or would not think of—at least, not right away.

My thoughts sifted every possible hideout from the Hanging Woman to the Powder, estimating their chances of getting to them.

I thought it more than likely they were close by. Without horses, which I doubted they had, they could not have gone far. Of course, there was always the chance they had horses saddled or were even in the saddle when the attack came.

On a hunch, I rode up the ridge toward Horse Creek Buttes.

There might be a dozen places of which I knew nothing, but I'd suddenly recalled that Philo had killed a grizzly that he'd trailed to a cave in the buttes. It was just a chance, but I had nothing else in the way of a lead.

The roan horse made good going of the mountain trails, even in the snow. The difference in elevation was only a few hundred feet, but the trails were none too good and the snow did not help.

First I led off as if riding back to the line cabin, for I might be trailed. There was a place on the North Fork of Lee Creek where I had rousted some cattle out of a hollow where they might be snowed in, and I rode by there, and trampled around in the snow, found a couple of steers and started them out, then cut into the brush and worked my way along the slope. Several times I drew up and studied my back trail.

The falling snow drew a veil across the distance, but within the area which I could survey there was no sign of pursuit. Nor did I really expect any. Woll and Ives were probably well on their way back to their own outfit by now.

The bear cave, when I found it scarcely an hour later, was empty. Yet somebody had prepared it for an extended stay, and some time before. A large pile of carefully cut wood was there, plenty of kindling, and on a rock shelf hacked out of the wall was a double row of canned goods, enough for a stay of at least a week, perhaps longer.

Philo Farley had been expecting trouble, or someone else had who knew of the cave.

All the time I was avoiding the memory of those leather-shod hoofs. The rider of that horse had been to Philo's outfit not once, but several times. Was it Farley himself? He looked too big a man for the weight that horse was carrying, but I could be wrong. Whenever those tracks came to mind I felt uneasy, almost scared.

Standing there in the cave, I tried to figure out where the two might be, but I could not. They were somewhere out there in the snow, a girl and a wounded man, perhaps even a dying one. And there was nothing I could do. To wander aimlessly about in the snow would do nothing but wear out my horse, and my chances of stumbling upon them were slight. Not knowing that I was hunting for them, they would have every reason to hide. Perhaps they would hide even from me.

I tore a sheet from my tally book and wrote a note, brief and to the point:

You can always come to me, no matter what.

What to sign it? This cave might be found by others, might even have been supplied by someone else. Whatever it was signed, it must be something

Philo would understand, and perhaps Ann would grasp too. So I signed it *Brennan on the Moor*.

That was the name of an old Irish folk song that Philo was often singing and which I'd asked him to sing a couple of times to me. He would make the connection at once, I was sure. And on our ride out from Miles City I had talked to Ann about the song, and about the highway-man about whom it was written.

Leaving the note where it could be quickly seen, I went outside, took a last look around, and walked my horse away, brushing out what tracks we left, knowing the snow would obliterate them that much the faster.

It was a long, cold ride back to the line camp. There were strange horses in the corral when I got there. I swung down and, rifle in hand, walked up to the door.

Eddie Holt sat inside, his back against the wall. He had a six-shooter belted on—the first time I'd seen him wear one—and his Winchester in his hands.

When I stepped into the room I found myself facing Bill Justin and three of his hands. All of them were men I knew, all of them men with whom I'd worked. But there was no friendliness in their faces, none at all.

"Hello, Mr. Justin," I said. "I wasn't expecting you out here in this weather."

He shifted his position uneasily. "Pike, I'm

going to have to let you go. Windy and Nebraska are going to take over."

"Mind giving me a reason?"

Justin hesitated. "There's been talk. You were seen driving cattle down into Wyoming."

"Whoever told you that," I said, "should have looked into it. They were your cattle. I trailed rustlers down there, and Eddie and me, we took them away from the rustlers, set them afoot, and came back here."

Justin looked uncomfortable, and then Nebraska spoke up. "You were mightly friendly with Tom Gatty," he said, "and we found tracks of his horse close by."

"He was a friend of mine. He did come here. He came here after a bottle of patent medicine. You know Tom . . . he's always dying."

Nobody said anything to that, so I said to Eddie, "All right, get packed. We're riding out of here." I glanced at Bill Justin. "Or do you want us to walk?"

Justin's face turned red. "No need to get nasty about it. Ride the horses and be damned."

"Mr. Justin," I said, and I spoke very carefully, "I want you to hear this clear, and the rest of you, too. And I want it told to the rest of the outfit. I never stole a cow in my life, and you damned well know it. I worked for the brand always, and worked hard for you.

"Now get this. I take it you are not calling us

thieves. You've only hinted at it. Well, I'm laying it on the line. If you, or anybody else, takes it on themselves to name me as a thief, you'd better go armed from there on in. I'm no gunfighter, and you all know it, but if one word is said to point me as a thief, I'll kill the man who said it, and every man who repeats it, as long as I last. Every damn one of you knows I never quit in my life, and you know I mean what I say."

Not one of them opened his mouth, and it was wise, for I was getting madder by the minute. Eddie, he got up and started putting our outfits together, but I never took my eyes off the men.

Then, because I felt sorry for Bill Justin, I said to him: "And something else. If you're tied in with Bohlen you'd better get shut of him and his vigilantes. They've attacked, maybe killed Philo Farley and his sister, and all hell is going to break loose."

"His sister?" Justin looked startled, shocked.

"I brought her out here . . . remember?"

Justin seemed frightened, and he started to bluster. "Farley was nothing but a damned nester . . . a cow thief. He—"

"Mr. Justin," I said, "Philo Farley was a former officer in the British Army. He belongs to one of the finest families in Great Britain. Philo Farley, in his own right, had money enough to buy you and sell you and never notice the difference. He'd no need to steal cows, or desire to. He just liked this country and the life here.

"Half the cattlemen and the money behind the others down in Wyoming are friends of his. Believe me, when this gets out the country won't be big enough to hold Bohlen and those tied in with him!"

Justin's face was dead white as I finished. Uneasy before, he was really scared now. He was never a bad man, but weak around Bohlen's bluster and power. I really was sorry for him, but I was glad I was through with him.

Windy came outside with us as we saddled up. I'd turned the roan into the corral and was taking that line-backed dun. The roan was used up, and the line-back was a good, tough horse.

"That true, what you said in there?" Windy asked.

"Sure."

He was silent for a couple of minutes, but as we stepped into our saddles, he said, "Pronto, if that's true, you'd better run and you'd better hide."

"What's that mean?"

"Why, you damned, bull-headed fool," he said softly, for Windy had always been a friendly man, "if that's true Bohlen will be hunting you. You'll be the only person who knew for sure about that sister of Farley's, and you'll be the only one who could point a finger at him. Pronto, if what you say is true, Roman Bohlen has got to kill you!"

Funny thing . . . he was right, and I'd never given it a thought. Not that way.

Frow now on, Bohlen would be hunting me. Not rustlers, not Farley, not anybody else but me.

After that, if Farley wasn't dead, he would have to kill him and hide the body.

And that meant he would have to kill Ann, too.

CHAPTER 12

I T WAS NIGHT and it was cold, and we had no more home than a busted poker chip. There at the end Bill Justin had got all upset and insisted we didn't have to leave at night, with it getting colder by the minute, but I had my neck bowed and would rather freeze to death than spend another night in that cabin.

It was worth leaving to see their faces when Eddie dumped all that bear sign into an empty burlap sack. Why, their faces were longer than a mule mare's; and Nebraska he almost reached for one of them, but Eddie picked up the meat cleaver.

"You go ahead, Mister Cowpuncher. You just pick that up and you'll find yourself liftin' a stub. You'll leave your hand right there on the table."

Nebraska was an ornery man, but he looked up at Eddie Holt and then at that cleaver and he was in no mind to take the chance. So we gathered up our things and lit out.

The snow crunched under our boots as we walked over to saddle up, but it wasn't until we were riding out that Eddie said, "You got a place to go? I mean, you got something in mind?"

First thing I thought of was that cave. There was grub there, shelter, and firewood, and there was a creek only a whoop and a holler down the canyon.

When we rode out from the place the snow was a good twelve inches deep on the level. Here and there where it could drift it was three or four times that deep, and no sign of easing off. All we needed now was a wind and we'd have a first-class blizzard. And unless a man has seen a blizzard in Montana or Dakota he hasn't seen anything.

Me, I was wearing a pair of wore-out shotgun chaps and I envied Eddie, who had him a pair of woolly chaps left over from his days with the Buffalo Bill Show. Not that others didn't wear them. A good many Montana cowhands went in for woolly or angora chaps for winter riding, but they'd always seemed a mite too fancy for me.

With my coat turned up around my ears and my hat tied down under my chin with a scarf, I surely didn't look the romantic picture folks have of a Montana cowhand, but I wasn't thinking of looks. I was thinking of that cave and wondering what Ann Farley was doing now—if she was alive.

My face grew stiff from the cold and my fingers were numb, even though I changed hands on the bridle to beat them in turn against my legs. Several times we got down and walked to keep our feet from freezing.

One satisfaction I had to keep me warm. Before leaving I had outlined the work we'd done to Justin and the men who were taking over from us, told them where we'd chopped holes in the ice, where the feed had been best, where the stock had taken to holing up in bad weather to get out of the wind, and generally giving them the layout.

"You did a lot of work," Justin had admitted grudgingly.

"Oh, sure!" I told him sarcastically. "Rustling cows doesn't take much time!"

A couple of times when we were standing in the shelter of trees, I studied the stars, not wanting to go too far north. The landmarks all looked different under the snow.

It was shading toward daylight when we finally scrambled into the canyon near Horse Creek Buttes and found the cave. It was empty.

We led our horses just inside the entrance. There the passage narrowed down, too small for a horse to go through, but it widened out beyond that point. There was shelter from the wind if not from the cold.

Inside, where there was a crack in the rock that was black from old fires, we built our own fire, and we made our beds on the cave floor, using the dried leaves and grass that someone—Philo, I believed—had prepared.

Neither of us felt like talking, and we weren't

hungry, so after a cup of coffee to warm us up, we turned in, rolling up in our blankets.

A startled movement from one of the horses woke me.

The coals glowed a deep red, so the fire could not long have burned down. Eddie was sleeping quietly . . . I could hear his steady breathing. And I could hear the restlessness of the horses. Something was out there . . . something that bothered them.

One hand reached out and grasped my Winchester, and then I eased up from my warm bed, and in my socks, I went through the passage. Very gently I put a hand on the shoulder of the nearest horse.

I worked my way carefully along and spoke softly in his ear. Then I went under his neck, under the neck of the next horse, and stood in the opening of the cave, looking out on the white expanse of the snow.

As I looked, something flopped in the snow, lunged a couple of paces, then flopped again. There was a muffled groan . . . then silence.

For a long minute, I waited. There was no further sound, no movement, but something was out there, something that must be a man.

Putting my Winchester down, I stepped out into the snow. In two swift strides I was beside him.

Bending over, I caught him by the collar and rolled him over on his back. The face was indistinguishable in the vague reflected light of the snow. Taking him by the collar, I dragged him to the shelter of the cave's mouth, then through the passage.

As I filled the passageway a handful of grass suddenly hit the fire, and I heard a gun hammer click back.

"Is that you, Pike?" Eddie's voice said.

"It's me," I answered. "I found something."

Eddie added fuel to the fire and when it blazed up, we stared down into the face of the injured man. It was Shorty Cones.

While Eddie built up the fire, I peeled back Shorty's clothes to see what was wrong. He had been shot twice in the back, and the two bullet holes were not two inches apart. The inside of his clothing was stiff with frozen blood, and of one thing I was sure. Only the cold had saved his life by causing the blood to coagulate, but I wasn't giving him much chance.

Eddie put his hand on my shoulder. "Pronto, you leave him to me. I helped doctor more than one hurt man."

Frankly, I was glad. Nobody was more scared than me when it came to tackling a thing like that. I had never had much to do with more than the sprains and bruises, and the occasional breaks a man can get on the range, but right off I could see that Eddie knew what he was about. Long before he'd gone to work for the Buffalo Bill Show he had been driving for a country doctor and had picked up a lot, helping him in a lot of ways.

So I made coffee and kept the fire going. And I dug out a bottle I had stashed away. Neither Eddie nor me was much on the liquor, and whiskey can be death to a man who's out on a cold night. A man full of whiskey will freeze to death faster than a sober man, for the liquor brings a temporary warmth, brings the heat to the surface of the skin, where it disappears into the cold air, leaving him colder than before. On the other hand, a man who has come in out of the cold can take a drink to warm himself up—if he isn't going out again.

After a few minutes Shorty began to mutter, and then his eyes opened. He looked up at Eddie, stared at him for several minutes, then turned his head and looked at me.

"Hello, Shorty," I said. "You just lie quiet. I'm making some coffee."

He seemed to relax, staring up into the darkness near the cave's roof where the firelight flickered, then his eyes closed.

After a moment, they opened again. "You find my horse?" he asked, speaking with surprising loudness.

"No. I'll go look." I tugged my boots on over my wet socks. "Shorty . . . who shot you?"

He looked puzzled. "*Shot? I'm shot?*" His brow puckered in a frown and his lips seemed to feel of the words before he spoke them. "I thought . . . something hit me . . . something . . . I don't know."

131

Eddie took up the bottle and touched it to Shorty's lips. "This here's whiskey."

I stood up, stamping my feet solid into my boots, and shrugging into my coat.

It was bitterly cold out there, and now the wind was blowing hard. In a way I was glad of it, for any tracks we or Shorty had left would be covered. No chance for Roman Bohlen, or anybody else, to find us.

Not fifty yards from where I'd found Shorty, his horse was standing with reins trailing. Evidently he had fallen from the saddle, or had fallen after he dismounted to find the cave. For it seemed obvious that he had known of it. It began to seem as if almost everybody knew of this cave.

Gathering up the reins, I led the horse to the cave mouth, then brushed off the snow.

Shorty had his eyes closed when I came in, packing his saddle. Eddie looked up at me.

"He talks wild now. Said something about meet-ing somebody . . . then about some shoot-ing at the Tower."

"He must mean Devil's Tower. It's down in the Bear Lodge Mountains or near them." Had Bohlen been down there, I wondered.

Leaning over him, I said, "Shorty, was Bohlen down there?"

"No," came the answer.

His eyes opened, and there for a minute or two he looked right into mine, as sane as I was myself. Then he turned his head and looked around, wonderingly.

"Pike," he said, "I made it, didn't I? I made the cave."

"Did you stock this place? With grub and firewood?"

"Hell, no!" He looked at me oddly. "How'd you know of this place? This is old Clyde Orum's hideout."

Clyde Orum! Why, I hadn't heard the name in years, or thought about him.

"Did you know him?" I said.

"Chin Baker did . . . and he's got family around. Chin knew something about them. We hid out here once . . . so when I had to run . . . I came for this place."

He seemed to be finding it hard to talk.

"Why did you run?" I asked.

He didn't answer for a moment, then he said, "Hell, Pike, the lot of us . . . they wiped us out. Just came out of nowhere and wiped us out . . . never seen any of them before."

Eddie came up, shaking his head at me. "I got you some soup, boy."

"Did they shoot you?"

"I'm shot?" he said again in that puzzled way. "I thought somebody hit me from behind, but there was nobody around except—"

But he didn't finish. Shorty wasn't going to need that soup.

Eddie slowly turned around and went back to the fire and put the bowl of soup down. Shorty Cones had died right while we talked to him, right in the middle of a sentence.

Nobody around except . . . *who?*

Somebody had shot Shorty Cones in the back, shot him at close range, somebody he knew but did not fear. It had been just the same with Johnny Ward.

And the Gatty outfit had been wiped out. Did that mean they had killed Tom too?

And who were *they?*

Discouragement and depression settled on me. Suddenly all I wanted in the world was to be out of here. Right then if I had been close to a railroad I would have caught me an armful of boxcars and left out of there. I'd have headed south to get away from the snow, and punched cows along the Mexican border the rest of my days.

I'd come here to spend a quiet winter caring for Justin cows, and I'd wound up getting fired from my job, accused of rustling cattle I'd ridden miles to save; and now a man I'd tried to help was dead, and the whole Gatty gang gone. Strangers were riding over the country killing folks without anybody knowing who they were, or even that it had happened.

That was the thing that troubled me. It was all pretty sly . . . if we hadn't come upon Shorty Cones before he died it might have been months, even years, before anybody knew anything at all about the Gatty gang being wiped out.

So what happened to that herd of cattle they had hid back in the hills? Right then I made a wild guess, and as soon as I made it I told myself it was true, even though a damned fool idea it was.

Eddie handed me a bowl of soup, and he ate the bowl he'd poured for Shorty. Neither of us looked at him.

"Eddie, we're going to leave out of here," I said. "We'll ride into Miles City or somewhere and catch us a train."

"All right."

When I finished my soup I put the bowl aside and wiped my mouth with the back of my hand. Eddie he was looking at me.

"What's eatin' you?" I asked.

"What about that Ann Farley? You going to leave it this way?"

Well, that did it. That put it right on the line, and he knew just as well as I did that in spite of all my talk I wasn't going any place without knowing what had happened to Ann Farley.

"Come daylight," I said, "we'll look around."

"Pronto," Eddie said gently, "it's daylight now. It's been daylight for a spell."

It was true, and with the realization of it I got to my feet and we packed our little gear and stuffed in our packs what we could of the supplies that remained, leaving a-plenty for whoever might come after.

In Shorty's pockets we found about thirty dollars, which I put into a worn envelope that contained a letter from his sister in Missouri. She would get the letter and what else there was. We took his horse for a pack animal, and left Shorty there.

"We haven't got a shovel, and the ground is frozen," Eddie said.

Suddenly my mind went to the note I'd left when I'd first visited the cave. Turning quickly, I caught Eddie by the arm.

"Did you see a bit of paper back there? A note?"

"Something fell to the floor . . . I don't know what it was."

Stepping past him, I went over to where I'd left my note and picked up the piece of paper lying there. It was my own note, but written across the bottom of it was something else:

The cabin of Kilworth.

Only that, but it was signed *Pedlar Brown*, and I needed no more.

When we had come riding up from Miles City and had left the Tongue, we had taken an old trail over Poker Jim Butte, and we'd seen a tumbled-down cabin. Ann had said it reminded her of some she'd seen in Ireland, in the Kilworth Mountains.

And it was the Kilworth Mountains from which Bold Brennan of the song had come, and Pedlar

Brown had been a man he'd robbed, who robbed him back, and they became partners.

So they had been here after all, but seeing the supplies, they had left, fearing to be found.

Ann had been here! Suddenly there was a singing inside me, and I went outside quickly.

"Mount up, Eddie," I said. "We've a ride to make!"

It was only five or six miles, but they would be long, long miles until I saw Ann Farley again, and knew that she was safe and well.

CHAPTER 13

AS WE TOOK the trail toward Poker Jim, I tried to study out what Shorty Cones had said. Their outfit had been wiped out by a bunch of strange riders who came on them so suddenly there was no chance to put up much of a fight.

Cones himself had not even realized he was shot, and he must not have realized how badly he was hurt.

And that last thing he had said? There was no one there except . . .

Except *who?* Somebody he had not expected to be dangerous to him. Somebody he had considered harmless, or somebody who was a friend.

"That cave, Eddie. I figured Farley had stocked that cave, but he didn't. That means somebody else did. And not Shorty, either."

"How about Baker? He knew of it."

Chin Baker was an old outlaw, and he had operated in this country for years. He was said to have run with Clyde Orum's gang, and he had known of the cave.

When we came upon the cabin on Poker Jim, it was half buried in snow. It sat back among the rocks, under some pines, not easily seen under normal circumstances, and under a fresh fall of snow almost perfectly hidden.

Our horses buck-jumped through the deep snow and into the trees, and when we reached the cabin we could see a few tracks around the door and out to the dug-out stable. Eddie took our horses, and I went up to the door and rapped.

Ann Farley opened it. She had a gun in her hand, and from the look in her eyes she wouldn't have hesitated to use it.

When she saw me the gun muzzle lowered. "You found us! I knew you would!"

She stepped aside and I bent my head to enter the low doorway. Many mountain cabins were built in a hurry by men short of materials, and sometimes the doorways were low like this one. But inside you stepped down several inches to the floor and there was standing room.

Across the room lay Philo Farley, stretched out on a bunk, and he looked bad, very bad.

He lifted a hand. "Pronto, I am glad you're here. Take care of her, will you?"

"I'll take care of you both," I said. "Eddie's out there, and Eddie's a hand with a wounded man. You wait, we'll have you up and about in no time."

"Take care of her—that's all I ask."

"Was it Roman Bohlen?"

He looked at me, and the expression in his eyes changed. "It was, . . . in person. He shot me when I was unarmed. He would have hung me if we hadn't escaped."

He gestured to indicate Ann. "She got me back into the house, just reached out and grabbed my collar and hauled me back inside. But then she proved to be smarter than I would have been, for she hurried me right across the room and out of the back window."

"We had our horses hidden back in the woods," Ann explained, "for we were all saddled and ready to ride to Miles City. I knew if they would shoot him down like that, they would continue the attack, and wouldn't hesitate to burn the house."

"Did they know you were a woman?"

"They may not have even seen me. No, I don't believe they knew."

Just then Eddie ducked through the low door, so I stepped back and waved him to Farley.

"What happened?" I asked Ann.

"By the time the house was burning, we were riding away. It was only a few feet from that rear window to the bushes."

Now, all my life I'd had a temper. Not that I ever

got mad when I was fighting, but it could explode into real trouble from time to time, which was the reason I kept a tight rein on it. In a fight there was no reason for being mad, and usually I fought only for fun. But now something curious was happening to me, and it scared me.

Turning away from Ann, I went outside into the day. There was a heavy overcast of gray cloud, but the snow made everything bright. I stood there, looking across the narrow canyon at the black trees, tufted with snow. For the first time in my life I was mad, with a cold, ugly anger that shocked me.

These people, and good people they were, had been shot at and hunted like wild animals. Their home had been burned, their belongings destroyed; and if they were found now they would be killed. And I, because I was with them and because I was myself suspected, would be killed too.

My hands were shaking, my whole body was quivering with fury, and I fought myself into calmness. At the same time that my fury gripped me, another part of me seemed to be standing by in surprise that this could be happening to me.

Suddenly I did not want to run. I did not want to get away. I wanted to hunt *them,* smash them, break them, show them what hatred could be. They had begun it; now they must accept the consequences.

A saner part of me kept warning me that nothing

was to be gained by such tactics; but another part of me was telling me that violence breeds violence, and that those men would not be content with what they had already done, but would strive to do more, to do worse. And I knew that when such men turn to violence they seem to seek out the weak and the helpless. Many a mob has been turned back by an armed and determined man, though that same man, unarmed, would have been destroyed without a thought.

When evil takes up violence, the good have no choice but to defend themselves.

Presently Ann came out and stood beside me.

"I knew you would come, Mr. Pike. I knew you would," she said.

"My name is Barnabas. But everybody calls me Pronto."

"I'll call you Barney." She paused. "I told Philo you would come."

"We've got to get him into Miles City," I said. "We can rig a travois, and in the snow the trip won't be too rough."

We talked there for a few minutes, and then she went back inside, and I walked off a few steps and stood under the trees, where I could watch both up and down the canyon. As I stood there, I tried to figure things out.

There was a party of would-be vigilantes out . . . maybe only Bohlen's outfit. They would be hunting Farley, and they would be hunting me.

There was also the bunch that shot up Gatty's rustlers, and I was sure they were a different crowd altogether.

And there was the rider who rode the horse with the leather shoes. And that rider was a cold-blooded killer who didn't seem to fit in anywhere.

All of those people were our enemies, all of them a danger to us. Under the circumstances, our only hope was to get into Miles City or some good-sized community where we could at least have the benefit of public opinion. Out here we could all be killed, buried, and after a short time forgotten. In town, right among folks, it would be an almighty great risk to try killing us. At least, it would be a big risk to try killing the Farleys.

But it was a long hard trip into Miles City, which lay a good many miles off to the north and east, and every mile of it a danger. We couldn't move as fast as a man riding free, but we could make fair time in the snow if we could rig a sled.

All the while I was standing there in the cold, I was watching for anyone coming our way, but the canyon was empty. And I knew the little smoke we made could not be seen outside the canyon, for by the time it had lifted that high it had faded out to nothing.

Eddie came out and stood beside me. "He's hurt bad, Pronto. Real bad."

"Could he stand a two-, three-day trip into Miles City?"

Eddie shrugged. "Maybe. I'd guess he couldn't, but that's a tough man in there."

He paused, then took out a couple of cigars. "Mr. Farley gave me these . . . have one." He lit up, and then asked, "Couldn't we make it no faster?"

When I shook my head, he asked, "Who is Lottie?"

"Lottie?"

"He talked about her some. I mean when he was delirious . . . he had a spell of it for a while."

"Somebody he knew back home, I reckon. I don't know of any Lottie around here."

While Eddie took a spell on watch, I went inside to drink some coffee and warm up. Also, I wanted my rifle, which I'd left inside, although I had the six-shooter belted to me.

Ann poured out coffee and handed it to me, along with a sandwich of bread and warmed-up meat.

"What are you going to do when this is over?" she asked.

"Homestead."

My answer came out so quick it surprised even me, but when I thought about it I knew that was what I was going to do. I was going to homestead on some good water and start my own outfit, and if they wanted to trouble me about it they could try. They wouldn't be picking on any amateur. I had been there before when it came to trouble.

"I want a place of my own," I said; "a ranch with some cattle and some good horses."

Now that I'd said it out in words, I knew the idea had been there all along. I even knew the place, and I'd only seen it one time, and that quite a while back. It was over against the Big Horns where the Lodge Grass headed up. It was rough country, but there was water, and I liked it.

We talked about it for a while, and Ann Farley surprised me by knowing quite a lot about range life. Of course, as she explained, Philo had written her of his own troubles and plans, as well as what was going on around him. But she knew more than that, and she told me she had talked to some of the Englishmen who had invested in Wyoming and Montana cattle, and had read something about it in the papers.

"There were some very good articles in the *Fortnightly Review*," she added, "written by men who had been over here. I was curious about what Philo was doing in Montana, so I tried to learn everything I could about it."

"You did a job," I admitted, surprised that anybody could learn that much about range conditions and cattle from books or magazines.

Later, when I went outside to relieve Eddie and to check on the horses, I thought about it a good deal. If a girl like that could learn something about such things by reading, I might learn something myself by studying. And if I was going to make something of myself, I'd better get down to brass tacks and do something about it.

"Nothing to see," Eddie said, "but man, I don't like the feel of it. I think we should get out."

"Tonight?"

Eddie was reluctant, but finally he said, "Better wait until almost daybreak. He's resting well in there, or was when I came out."

"He still is."

"He can use it." He looked at me. "Why don't we make a sled? I brought an axe along and I noticed an adze there in the cabin. She ain't much account, but I could sharpen it up a mite."

"Are you any good with an axe?"

"I'm a fair hand," Eddie admitted, "but I've noticed you cutting wood. You'll do."

"I grew up with an axe in my hand," I said. "All right, sled it is. I'll take the axe and go hunt some runners."

Taking the rifle and the axe, I went up the hill into a young stand of lodge-pole pine, and picked a couple of slim young trees and cut them down. Back at the cabin we smoothed off the bark and with the adze cut a flat surface to slide on.

Eddie was a better hand than me. He showed he had some knowledge of such things, and he had skill with his hands. Like I've always said, I could do any work that could be done from the back of a cow pony. Otherwise, I wasn't much account.

Yet if I decided to homestead I'd have to do all kinds of work, I'd have to build my own cabin, even plow a mite to put in a home garden. But first off, I'd need some cattle and a couple of horses.

Every few minutes while I was working I looked around and studied the country, and I was getting the same feeling Eddie had, the itch to be away from here. The place had an eerie feel to it, added to by the ghostly white of everything under the new fall of snow.

Maybe it was because I was expecting trouble, expecting Roman Bohlen and his outfit to catch up with us, or even that other crowd, the bunch who had shot up Tom Gatty's rustlers . . . these things going on in that country made a man uneasy.

All the while in the back of my mind was the nagging thought that I had a showdown coming with Bohlen. It had to come, but I couldn't see how I could win. He had the money, the influence, the men back of him; and in a fight he was a whole lot bigger than me.

"I wish we could have boxed more," I told Eddie. "I surely wish we had."

"You learned a lot," Eddie said. "You took to it. You just remember what you learned and you won't have any trouble. You're a natural. Believe me, if you'd started younger you could have made it; but a man should start boxing when he's young."

Philo Farley slept the day through, and most of the night. Toward daylight, when I was in the cabin drinking coffee, he woke up and lay with his eyes open. Ann was wrapped up in her blankets, fast asleep.

"Pike? Is that you?" Farley said.

I walked over and sat down on the edge of the bunk. "You want some soup or something?" I asked. "We've got some ready."

"Not just yet." He stayed quiet for a minute. "Pike, is Ann asleep?"

When I nodded, he said, "She should never have come out here, but she was always like that. She loved to climb in the mountains back home, and to ride the wildest horses. Ann should have been born in Montana, not Ireland."

He was quiet again, and I told him of our plans to get him into Miles City. He listened, then nodded slightly. "You can try. It will get Ann there, anyway. But I won't make it, Pike, I am sure I won't."

"That's a fool way to talk!"

"I've got the feeling, Pike." He looked at me curiously. "You take good care of Ann. She belongs in this country."

"She'll be going home."

He turned his head slowly from side to side. "She might, but I don't believe it. She's very like me, Pike. She's seen those Big Horns against the sky, and she has ridden over the range. I think she'll stay."

He gave me a sudden sharp look. "You know, Pike, living out here gives a man different standards. Over there, education and position seem the most important things, but out here . . . well, it's the way it should be everywhere—character comes first. Not that a man should underrate either education or position. But it is the man that matters, not where he came from or where he went to school.

"Take you, Pike. I don't know anything about your blood lines and I care less, but you've got what this country needs—what it will always need. You've got stamina, courage, and a strong sense of justice."

I was kind of surprised and embarrassed. I went over and knelt beside the fire, where I dished up a cup of soup for him, and I helped him to it.

He looked up at me. "I'd like to make it to Miles City. I'd like to recover, Pike. If I do, I'll kill Roman Bohlen."

"He needs it," I agreed, "but this country is outgrowing that way. Maybe that time is already past and Bohlen himself didn't know. He's gone too far this time."

Just short of daybreak I went up into the woods to get their horses, and led them back down. We hitched our pack horse to the sled, and the rest of our gear we put on their extra horses. Eddie got up in the saddle to lead off.

It wasn't until I was helping Ann into her saddle that I noticed the tracks of her horse.

When I looked at its hoofs I saw that it wore leather Indian-style shoes.

CHAPTER 14

BY THE TIME the sun came up we were crossing a shoulder of the mountain near Padget Creek, and when we actually caught sight of the sun we were already down in the valley of the Otter. It wasn't easy going, but by taking turns at scouting ahead and breaking trail, Eddie and me found our way. We took our nooning on Ten Mile Creek, and since then we had come a mite further.

"How's it going?" I asked Philo.

"All right," he said quietly.

He looked drawn and pale, and I knew he was taking a beating on this trip. If he lived through this, he'd be almighty lucky; but he would have died anyway without proper care. Or he would have been hung or murdered if he was found. We had no choice but to make the try.

We poured him a cup of coffee, and I squatted alongside him while he drank it. It was strong enough to peel paint off a barn, and it seemed to do him good.

But there was something troubling me, and I could not ride easy without trying to learn what I could.

"Too bad," I said, "about Johnny Ward."

He was looking right at me when I said it, and there wasn't so much as a flicker in his eyes. "Johnny Ward? Who was he?"

"Cowpoke," I said. "Nice kid." I sipped my coffee. "Somebody shot him. Somebody he knew well enough not to be scared. Shot him in the back at close range."

"That's rotten," he said. "It's a miserable way to go."

He tried to stretch out a little more and a spasm of pain crossed his face.

"Shorty Cones is dead, too. He got to us before he died. He was shot the same way."

"Cones? Wasn't he a kind of bad one? I believe he used to be around John Chinnick's place with that outfit."

"Uh-huh."

If Philo Farley knew anything at all about the death of either man, he was better at hiding it than I would have believed. It worried me, for of one thing I was very sure. Philo Farley knew the murderer, and Philo must have been friendly to him or those tracks would not have been seen at his place—not so many, from so many different occasions. And whoever the murderer was, he was dangerous to know.

Who could it be who had known all three—Johnny Ward, Cones, and Farley? Who was accepted on familiar terms by all of them?

"Had many visitors lately?" I asked.

Farley had closed his eyes. "No . . . very few."

He looked bad, so I stopped bothering him.

We mounted up again and I led off. The trail

along Otter Creek was good, for some cattle had used it, and at least one rider—I could not make out the tracks.

"Will they follow us?" Ann asked. "Bohlen, I mean?"

"Yes."

"And if they catch us they will kill you too?"

"They'll try."

Both Eddie and me kept our heads turning, not only to look back, but around us and ahead too. That mysterious killer was worrying both of us, for nothing about it fitted in, anywhere.

"It's got to be somebody we don't know," I had told him during a moment together, "somebody we don't even suspect."

"Somebody nobody suspected," he said, "looking at the way they were killed."

The day was cold, but it had cleared off and the sky was bright, the snow sparkled in the sunlight, the pines even seemed green instead of black. The going was hard on Farley, but there was no help for it. Part of the time, when the trail was good, we moved at a trot. Actually, there were fewer bumps than one would have expected, and he rode well.

As we rode, I tried to figure out the trail ahead. By this time they were following us, or else we had no reason to worry that they ever would. If they followed us they would have an easy trail for part of the way, but the sun was warming the air a little, and that little would help us. It would not be warm enough to melt the snow much, but it would melt the tracks a little around the edges and make them impossible to identify. And that would be enough to make it harder to find us.

We made a rough, quick camp on Three Mile Creek and I went out to smear as much of our trail as I could before the melting stopped and it started to freeze, which would be before long.

The wind had started to rise, and the air was already colder.

South of Three Mile Creek there was a ridge that pointed toward the meeting of Three Mile with Otter. King Mountain was off to the west. I rode up on the ridge and drew rein in a sort of notch where my horse would not offer an outline against the sky. The sun was in my eyes when I first topped out on the ridge, but I waited there, turning my collar up against the wind and watching up the stream and across it.

We had left the trail that followed the Otter some distance back, crossing to the east side of the creek. Now, plain as the Big Horns against a far-off sky, I saw the riders come, single file. There were nine of them by count. They rode on down the creek, past the mouth of Three Mile, and far below they seemed to veer east, and then I lost them from sight. But I was sure they were Bohlen's men.

Turning my horse, I started back. My horse made almost no sound on the snow, and when the rider came out of the gulch below me, not more than fifty yards off, I wasn't seen. It was a woman in a man's rough clothes, riding a mule!

She wore old overalls of the bib kind that you see mighty rarely in cow country, and she had on a beat-up old sheepskin coat and a battered hat. At first glimpse I thought it was Calamity Jane, who was one of the least attractive women I ever saw, and who dressed like that when she was freighting. But this woman was bigger. Only thing that made me sure she was a woman at that distance was her hair. It was nearly the color of Ann Farley's, a kind of auburn, and it was done in two thick braids.

All of a sudden she turned her head and looked right at me, and I said, "Howdy, ma'am!"

She just went on looking at me, no more expression on her face than on a ewe sheep, but her eyes flicked back of me once to see if I was alone.

"You seen a party of folks? Four, five of them?" she said.

"Yes, ma'am. I just saw them over yonder. Across the creek."

There was a flicker of impatience in her eyes. "Not them. This lot would have a woman with them . . . a young woman."

Something in the way she said *young woman* that decided me against telling, though I was not of a mind to tell anybody anything, the way things were.

When I said nothing, she went on, "How would somebody get across the mountain up ahead . . . Cook Mountain, ain't it?"

"You foller down Otter to the East Fork," I said. "It's the third creek on the east bank. The trail runs right alongside. You cross the east end of the mountain and hit the trail along Pumpkin Creek."

She looked at me a minute without saying a word, and then she rode off down the mountain. Glancing down at her mule's tracks, I saw them clear and neat. Small, neat hoofs had made a clearly defined track.

She was nobody I had ever seen before, but she spooked me, with her coming out of nowhere like that, and the odd way she had.

For a while I watched her ride down the mountain, and then I went over and headed down toward Otter Creek and the trail Bohlen's men had followed. I was taking a roundabout route, but I realized that the sooner I got back the better, for they might have passed close enough to camp to smell smoke, though I thought they seemed well beyond it.

After I reached the trail I saw the strange woman's mule's tracks proceeding right along the trail, so I cut across and went to our camp on Three Mile. It was shading into dark when I got back.

Ann was drawn-looking as she sat beside her brother, who was unconscious or asleep. Eddie, his eyes heavy from lack of sleep, came over to me as I stripped the saddle from my horse.

"He's in bad shape," he said. "I don't know whether he'll last or not."

I stood there with my hands resting on the horse, feeling as low as ever I had in my born days. This was a man I had liked. We'd never talked much. We'd never spent a lot of time together, but there'd been some nameless kind of sympathy between us. He was the sort of man who, if you were caught in a tight spot, you'd never think to look around at—you'd just know he was there, doing what ought to be done.

Eddie handed me a cup when we moved over to the fire and I burned my mouth and throat gulping the hot coffee. But after the coffee and some boiled beef, I felt better, and I told them about seeing that party of Bohlen's men.

"Won't be long," I said, "until they realize they're ahead of us. Then they'll sit down and wait."

"It's a big country," was Eddie's only comment.

It wasn't that big. Unless we took a long sweep around the Cook Mountains, there were only two trails across that I knew of, and one of them I'd just advised that strange woman to take. That was the trail most used, and more than likely that was where Bohlen and his men would wait for us.

Another, shorter trail, and a much tougher one, went over a saddle at the west end of the mountains, and then down Bridegroom Creek. I decided that was the one we'd best take.

"Get some sleep, Eddie," I said. "I'll wake you up at midnight."

Ann came to the fire after he'd curled up in his blankets. When I described to her the woman I'd met on the trail, she exclaimed, "Why, that's the woman who threw away the beans!"

She explained that. "It was the day after you left me at Philo's. He was asleep inside the cabin. I heard someone coming, and when I looked out, this woman was riding into the yard carrying a covered pot. I stepped outside the door to say hello, and she took one look at me and threw the pot on the ground. Then she turned around and rode away. I called after her, but she didn't stop. When I went out there, I found it was a crock of baked beans. She had thrown them out on the ground."

I chuckled, and Ann glanced at me kind of sharp. "Is that amusing?"

"Sure. She's just some woman who dotes on your brother. Plain as the horn on a saddle."

"You mean that when she saw me she thought I was some other woman of Philo's?"

"What else?"

WHEN AT LAST I got a chance to sleep, I slept like the dead, and Eddie had to shake me several times before he got me awake. It was the first time I could remember that I'd slept like that, for I'm by nature a light sleeper and an early riser.

"Everything all right?" I asked.

Eddie shrugged. "He's awake. He looks better.

He talks better. Pronto, if we could get that man to a doctor we could save him yet. I just know we could."

"We'll do it."

"Somebody was prowlin' about last night. Somebody who spooked the horses a time or two."

I pulled on my boots and stamped into them, and then reached for my coat. I checked my pistol and my rifle, and on a sudden hunch, stuffed my pockets with rifle cartridges.

"We've got to figure on trouble, Ann," I said as she came up. "We've got three days to go, traveling the way we are, and somewhere in those three days they will be wanting to kill us all. For if we reach Miles City and tell about the attack on your brother and you, Roman Bohlen won't have a friend from here to Cheyenne."

Our horses were in bad shape, for the feed had been poor. We had left with a little corn, but that was gone now, and if they lasted to Miles City we'd be lucky.

By high noon we were atop the pass that crossed the saddle to the head of Bridegroom Creek, and we paused there for a breather.

The air was crisp and cold, but pleasant. The horses were steaming from the tough climb. Ann came up beside me and we sat our horses looking out over the broken, half-forested country, crossed by several creeks.

"I still say it's a lovely land," Ann said. "I could live here forever!"

"They have a saying that it's hell on horses and women."

"It may be that, but I've a fondness for it, and as for Philo, he's actually thriving on it. He's getting better. Now he wants to ride a horse—he says we could go that much the faster."

Just then snow fell from a pine branch some distance up the slope. *"Look out!"* I yelled, and grabbed Ann around the waist and leaped my horse into the rocks and brush.

A blast of rifle fire raked the spot where we'd been, and up the slope I heard Bohlen's voice. "Get them! Get every damned one of them!"

I dropped Ann as I left the saddle, and when I hit the ground I lit running, rifle in hand. I turned and, crouching, ran to get hold of the trace-chains we'd hooked to the sled.

Philo was lying there, his face white but his eyes lit with a hard fire. "Hand me down a rifle," he said. "I'll not be done out of this."

Eddie was nowhere in sight; one horse was down and dying. They had trapped us for fair.

CHAPTER 15

PHILO LAY IN the trail, his sled hitched to a dying horse. Unhooking the trace-chains, I dug in my heels and dragged the sled back under the brush.

On our west a peak some two to three hundred feet high lifted above the trail, while on the east side it broke back more gradually, and there was a tumble of boulders, brush, and fallen trees, the latter a left-over from some by-gone landslip. It was among these we had taken refuge.

"Ann, get him off that sled and down in there." I indicated a dark hole where logs had fallen across some boulders and brush had grown up around. "And get all the blankets and grub."

Working my way into a crack among the rocks that gave me a view of the slope above, I waited. Though I was never a fast hand with a six-shooter, I'd stack up with anybody I ever saw with a rifle. But I'd never had to shoot at a man to kill, except some Indians, long ago.

Common sense told me we were finished. We just weren't going to get out of this. At the same time my own stubborn nature wouldn't let me do anything but bow my neck and try. I could no more quit than I could spread wings and fly out of there.

Suddenly, on the slope far above, a rider appeared. He was working his way down toward us, sliding his horse, and he was in sight just for the time it takes for a good long breath. Only I had been expecting him. The rifle came up in one easy movement, and I squeezed off my shot as my sights registered on him.

He was a good four hundred yards off, but he jerked, kind of twisted in the saddle, and fell, his head toward the horse's heels, his foot caught in the stirrup.

It seemed like they all shot at once then, and well they did, for it gave me a chance to locate my trouble; and believe me, it was all around.

Of a sudden there was a rush of boots on gravel, and when I turned to shoot there was Eddie. He had a raw furrow across the side of his cheekbone where a bullet had bled him, and there was blood on the side of his shirt.

"You hit bad?"

"Not so bad as I'll hurt walkin' all the way to Miles City. My horse took off a-runnin'."

Up the slope there was an occasional sound. Obviously they were working in around us to cut off any retreat; if we figured to try to get out, now was the time. If they got us pinned in here, they could keep us until hell froze over and the devil had icicles in his beard.

Behind us was a slanting wall of rock that sloped back steeply for thirty or forty feet to level ground above. On our left the trail dipped down, winding down the mountain toward the head of Bridegroom Creek. In front of us were huge slab-like boulders, and the space between them and the wall behind us varied from three to maybe twelve feet, much of it covered over by logs and debris. At the far end, away from the trail, where Ann and Philo had gone, was that sort of cave under the logs and fallen rock.

Eddie and me went in, and found Philo lying on the ground, several feet back, but Ann was gone.

"You all right?" I asked.

"All right?" He smiled at me. "How could I be all right? Ann's gone to look for a way out." He indicated an opening toward the back, on the downhill side, and when I went back and looked down I could see a crevice in the rocks down which water had run at some time or other.

It opened into a deep canyon, if you could call it that, not over six or eight feet wide, and a wild, unholy-looking place it was. Along the edge there was a sort of trail made by deer or elk, barely wide enough for them to set their feet. The gorge was partly shielded from above by trees and brush growing out of the walls and along the top.

Just as I was about to start down looking for Ann, she came climbing back up. "It's a way out," she said. "There's a brook down there . . . or a creek, as you call it, running due north."

"Eddie, you help Ann get Philo on a horse," I said. "He's in no shape to ride, but if he stays here he won't be in any shape to walk or even crawl, so he'd better try it. Then you start down the creek, but keep a lookout."

"What about you?" Ann asked.

"I'll hang back for a bit. Make 'em think we're dug in to fight it out."

It was almighty quiet there after they'd left. The only sound was the wind in the pines. The air was all vibrant and dancing, the way it is sometimes when the snow is melting. Once, back up the slope, I heard a pine cone fall. But there was no other sound for a long time.

Just when I was getting worried about the others, I heard the sound of a man sliding in gravel, and the next minute a head and shoulders stuck over the sloping rock behind me. I was squatting down against the boulders on the other side and when his head came over, my rifle came up and his eyes found me a split second before the bullet took the top of his head off.

He let go of everything and spilled over the rock, then slowly came full into sight, his rifle still gripped in his hand.

He slid to the bottom of the slope and I walked over and picked up his rifle, then peeled off his gunbelt and hand gun. He had another cartridge belt looped over one shoulder and under the other arm, so I took that too. Before this shindig was over I might need all the ammunition I could get.

After a minute a voice called, "Al?"

"You want him," I called back, "you come an' get him."

Somebody swore, and then I heard Bohlen. "Pike, you're a damned fool! Why fight us? You'll never work another day in this country, and you know it. Now, you come on up here and I'll give you fifty dollars and you can ride out of the country, nobody the wiser."

"Don't you miss any meals waitin' for me, Roman," I said cheerfully. "You may get me, but it's going to cost you. Why, we've got two of your men now. Leaves seven, doesn't it?"

Shifting my position a little, I backed toward the cave. It was time to give Bohlen something to worry about, something other than what would result if any of us got away.

"Hear about Gatty?" I called out conversationally. "We found Shorty Cones all shot up. Some big rustler outfit came and cleaned them out, lock, stock, an' barrel."

"Serves 'em right!" Bohlen was closer now.

"You mean you want an outfit that tough for neighbors? Listen, Roman, that Tom Gatty was no pilgrim. If that outfit wiped them out, what will they do to your stock? Why, I'd lay a bet they're sweeping your range right now! You won't have enough beef left to buy a cigar."

"Like hell!"

"Figure it for yourself. You've got nobody at the ranch. They'll clean you from hell to breakfast!"

A shot smashed into the logs not far from where I was, so I shot back, then yelled: "You talk to yourself, d'you hear? I'm through talkin' . . . but I'll laugh at you when you can't even hire a lawyer to keep you from hanging!"

Ducking back into the cave, I ran to the back and scrambled swiftly and silently down the deep, narrow crevice in the rock.

The others had made good time. I had to run and walk almost two miles before I caught up with them. Farley looked like a ghost, sitting up there on that horse, but he was game. He gave me a feeble grin and said, "I knew you'd make it, Pike. What happened?"

Glancing ahead to where Ann rode, I lowered my voice. "We've two less to worry about."

We had only three horses now, and one of us had to travel afoot, which was what I was doing. Not that I liked it. Me, I was a cowhand, and no cowhand will walk across a street if he can ride. Not that I hadn't done a sight of walking, time to time.

Still we made good time. The country was not so rough now, and though avoiding the regular trail we could still keep to pretty good going.

It was long after dark before I led them into a hollow in the mountains to camp. After it was dark I'd turned at right angles and gone due east into rough country by a little-known route that I'd followed a time or two. From here on I knew the country somewhat better, and the hollow in which we camped was not likely to be found, unless in the daylight.

All of us were all in, so we took a chance and built a small fire in the hollow among some boulders and fixed us a hot meal, although we were running short on everything but coffee. When we had eaten I smothered the fire and crawled back under the brush to rest. Eddie needed rest as much as I did, and this time we left to our broncs the job of keeping guard. They were not long from the wilds, and they would be apt to warn us of trouble. Nevertheless, I woke up twice during the night and prowled around, talking quietly to the horses and listening into the night, but I heard nothing.

By the time the sun was topping out on the Black Hills over east beyond the Powder, I was high up on a ridge of the mountain studying the country behind us.

The air was clear and sharp, and I saw them at almost the first glance. They were miles off, north of Beaver Creek, and raising angry dust at us. They must have missed our right-angle turn, and were hunting tracks where we hadn't made any.

By the time I came down off the mountain everybody was packed and ready to go.

Farley reached into a saddlebag. "Did you ever wear moccasins, Pike? They'll beat those boots for hiking or running."

They were almost a perfect fit, and they surely felt good. Farley wasn't the first rider I'd known who packed a pair of moccasins for wear around camp, though it wasn't the usual thing. I'd seen him wearing moccasins around his cabin a time or two.

Ann rode alongside me, and I let her carry my rifle, making that much less weight for me.

We nooned in a shallow place among low grass hills, with no trees around and no water but what we carried in our one canteen. There was a trickle of water in a creek bed and Eddie led the horses there to water, a good hundred yards off, while we brewed coffee on a buffalo-chip fire.

Nobody was talking. I still was dead beat, and so were the others. We drank our coffee and dowsed our fire, and when Eddie came back Farley was asleep or passed out, I couldn't tell which. Ann sat close to him, still sipping her coffee.

"We ain't going to make it this way," I said. "I'm about beat up from hiking and running." I took a swallow of coffee. "Eddie, you got to take Farley and Ann on into Miles City."

They just looked at me, too tired to ask the obvious question. "I'm going to get me a horse," I said. "I'm through walking. I'm going to get it from them, and I'm going to make a try at setting them afoot."

"You'll get killed," Ann said. "And you'd not be in this at all, neither of you would, if it hadn't been for us."

Me, I wasn't paying any attention. All the time

I'd been running along on sore feet I'd been get-ting madder by the minute, and now I was really ready for trouble, and I wasn't about to wait for it. I'd been chased about as far as I was going to run, and if they wanted a fight they were going to get it.

If I had to take on that whole crowd to get me a horse, then I'd take them on.

The sky was gray again, and it looked like more snow, and we were still a good distance from Miles City. "You go along," I said. "I'm going to make me a fight."

Eddie looked at me without speaking. He wanted to be with me, I knew that, but somebody had to care for Philo, and somebody had to keep them moving.

So I took a stick and laid it out for them. "You keep going due north," I said, "and you can't miss it. Over east is Pumpkin Creek, but she bends kind of wide toward the east, so don't waste around trying to follow it. You just keep north. Somewhere up yonder you'll have to cross the Pumpkin or the Tongue, but there's a crossing near where they join up. Try for that and cross over and go on into Miles City."

Eddie went to get the horses and I checked my rifle. Ann stood there, looking big-eyed at me, almost as if maybe she wasn't going to see me anymore—and maybe she wasn't.

Right then my muscles were sore, my feet were blistered, and my mind was all in a bind with stubbornness. It was the meanness in me that made me want to wait, just as much as it was wanting to give them a running start toward Miles City. If I could get at Bohlen's horses, or even hold his men up for a few hours, the others might make it on in. Otherwise it was going to be a fight all the way into town.

"Ann," I said, "Philo's got a chance. It's up to you and Eddie to get him there. I'm going to hang back and stir up trouble. You go along now."

She stood there, a serious smile on her face. "Barney," she said, "I think you're the finest, most genuine man I ever knew!"

That's a hell of a thing to say to a man. I felt my neck getting red and hunted around for words. But I couldn't find any that wouldn't make me sound more of a fool than I was.

"You better get goin'," I said. "Get your brother ready to start."

"If we come out of this, Barney, I'm going to stay in Montana."

"This is no place for an English lady."

"But I'm Irish, Barney, and you'll find the Irish all over the world, the men and the women too. I'm one of a family who have had cousins who fought in the French Army, in the Spanish Army, and in India. I had a second cousin who was killed with Custer—that's not very far from here, you said."

"There's nothing here for you," I said. "This is a rough country."

"Nothing for me? I think there is."

Me, I pulled my beat-up old hat down over my eyes and looked at my Winchester.

"You get to Miles City," I said, "and you tell them what happened out here. Tell them about those other killings too. And Ann—"

"What?"

"Don't you turn your back to anybody. *Anybody at all.* You hear?"

Eddie came up with the horses and I helped her get Philo into the saddle. He was drawn finer than any man I ever saw who was still alive and able to move.

"Luck, Pike," he said in a low voice, "the best of luck, man."

When Ann's horse started to turn away, she suddenly reached over and touched my cheek.

Eddie hesitated a moment longer. "I'll do the best I can," he said quietly. "You keep your hands up, boy. Don't you let them feint you out of position."

He rode off and I stood there, looking after them, and now that I felt I was seeing her for the last time, I finally admitted that I was in love with Ann Farley.

But there was no way it could do me a bit of good.

CHAPTER 16

A MAN HAS TO face up to himself sometime or other. You can go on being satisfied or ducking the issue only so long, and then there comes a time when you start asking yourself, not what you've done with your summer's wages, but with your whole life up to that minute. And more often than not the answer you have to give yourself isn't a happy one.

The thing a man has to realize is that it is never too late. I've known of many a man who has braced up and made something of himself after he was forty, with nothing to show for the years before that but scars and the cluttering up of dead wishes. About the worst thing a man can do is to let a dream die.

A while back, when I wasn't much more than a youngster, I used to think often of having my own place, and of just how I'd handle it. An idea like that in your mind doesn't just lie fallow; it builds up and gathers background, trying to fit itself for realization. Here and there you pick up a thought or an idea, you work for somebody else who does things well or badly, and you add to your little stock of information, and you do it mostly without thinking.

You get to studying range conditions, and the effects of different kinds of grass or forage, and all the while you are learning. Every idea is a seed and, like a seed, it germinates. Only you have to feed it to make it grow properly. My trouble was that after a lot of years of thinking, I'd sort of fallen into the rut of working for the other guy, of riding into town, having myself a time, fighting somebody who was supposed to be tough, and riding back home to do the same thing. The idea was still there, but it was growing in a mighty spindly fashion.

A man never starts to get old until he starts to forget his dream. Somebody said once that nature abhors a vacuum; well, from all I'd seen, I would say that nature dislikes anything that doesn't produce. And me? Maybe this was my time to die, because so far as I could recall I'd produced nothing but a day's work for a day's pay, I'd been honest, hard-working; I'd paid no attention to rain, snow or hail, I'd done my job, breaking the rough ones, pulling ornery steers out of bogs, eating the dust of roundups and the bawling sounds of roundup cattle on drives.

Only my dream wasn't dead. Until a few days ago it had just been lying there, starving for lack of hope. In a sort of way Ann made it come alive. There was never a thought in my mind that she was for me. She had breeding, education, a background suited to a woman like her. Philo was a tough, strong man who had to be somewhere to use his toughness and his strength, but Ann . . . ?

171

I was thinking about these things, but at the same time I was realizing that they would have picked up our trail by now and they would be coming on. They would make pretty good time, in spite of the fact that their horses would be showing the wear and tear of hard riding, too.

The place I'd picked for a stand wasn't much, just a buffalo wallow without much shelter, and they could ride around me and leave me sitting without ever knowing I was there unless I opened fire. Yet I had a hunch they would hold to what trail we had left and would come up to the stream right near by, and they would stop there for the night, or at least for a rest. It was an easy camp, a far more likely place than where we had stopped, for we'd had to think of hiding our fire.

Not that I didn't still have a chance if they continued on, for I could still walk. And in fact, over many miles, a man can walk down a horse—it has been done.

But I felt sure they would stop. Their horses must be badly beat, their grazing had been poor, and they had been ridden hard even before Bohlen started after us. And if they did stop, I would have one of their horses.

All my life I'd been fighting one way or other, and here and there I'd used my brains, such as they were. Mostly I'd just waded in swinging, and the thing that kept me winning—for I'd won ninety per cent of my fights—was simply that I'd never been willing to realize when I was licked. A time or two it had seemed like it, only something kept me swinging and I'd finally won.

It wouldn't be that way this time. This was a shooting matter. These men wanted to kill me . . . or some of them did . . . and they had to kill me.

So I waited, sitting there in my dusty clothes, needing a wash and a bite of food. And I figured my chances were down to nothing.

The sun was warm, there was a dark edging of wet earth around the patches of snow, but the melting had about let up for the time being. Evening wasn't far off, but it was still clear in the west where the sun was setting. All of a sudden, sitting there alone in the stillness, all the tiredness that had been piling up for days swept over me.

My eyelids grew heavy, and my muscles sagged. It felt comfortable, sitting there in the waning sun. The slight breeze was cool, but not unpleasant. I stood up and looked all around, but there was nothing in sight. Sitting down again, I made myself comfortable against the side of the wallow.

How long had we been running? How long since I'd had a full night of sleep? When all of this was over, if I was still alive, I was going to sleep for a week. But I had to stay awake now, for they would be coming at any time.

Again I stood up and looked carefully around. Nothing . . . nothing in sight, anywhere. Soon it would be getting dark. I sat down, and dug through my pockets, hunting for the stub of an old cigar, but I didn't find one. Hunching deeper into my coat, I waited.

Suppose they did not follow our tracks, but went on and laid an ambush somewhere up the trail? It was possible, but not probable, I thought.

My eyes were tired . . . I'd close them for just an instant.

I was half asleep when the rush of hoofs brought me up with a start and I lunged to my feet. A loop sailed out of nowhere and whipped around me, jerking taut as the horse sat back hard on his haunches. A second rope slapped me in the face as it circled my throat.

"Hold him like that." Roman Bohlen swung down from his saddle, drawing on a pair of heavy gauntlets. He was smiling as he walked toward me.

The others sat their horses, their faces expressionless. I'd worked with several of them, and one of the men who had a rope on me was Red Hardeman, a tough cowpuncher whom I'd whipped in a brutal fight at a dance a couple of years back. He had no reason to like me.

"I was expecting you to lay back and wait for us, Pike, because you're a damned fool. Now I'm going to give you something you've needed for a long time, and then we're going to catch up with the rest of that crowd and make an end of this."

The ropes held me tight. I was wearing my sheepskin coat, which impeded movement anyway, and the ropes had pinned my arms to my side and had a strangle on my neck.

Roman Bohlen was a big man, and strong. As he walked up to me he had the nastiest expression I've ever seen on a man's face. He drew back his gauntleted fist, and then he drove it at my face, but Eddie Holt's training had been good. Without even thinking about it, I pulled my head aside and the punch skimmed by.

Bohlen fell against me, and then he jerked back as if he'd gone crazy mad and started slamming me with both hands. He hit me once and my head rocked, then he hit me again. Deliberately, I braced my feet and stood there, determined not to go down. He struck me once more, then he tripped me, and when I fell he kicked me in the ribs again and again. Only that heavy coat kept him from smashing my side in.

How long he kept it up I had no idea. At first the blows stunned and hurt, then I became half sick with pain, and after that I was almost numb to the blows that followed. Yet I kept my senses. Finally, arm-weary, he stopped and stepped back, his hands hanging.

"All right, take your ropes off!" he said, and kicked me again in the side.

"Pike!" he yelled at me, and when I fought to reply, I couldn't, for my lips were smashed and my jaw swollen.

But he had turned away. "The hell with him!" he

said. "Let's get out of here. This one isn't important, anyway."

The saddle creaked as he mounted. "Red, you've hated his guts for a long time. I leave it to you. *Kill him!*"

Vaguely, I heard the pound of the hoofs as they rode off, and I forced my eyes open and looked up.

Red Hardeman sat his horse not fifteen feet away, and he held his Colt in his hand. I know he was thinking of the beating I'd given him, and of how we had never had any use for each other. And now he had me cold-turkey, and helpless.

"I'll say this for you," he said, "you got guts."

He lifted his pistol and laid the sights on my head, and he held them there. I didn't have strength enough to move, and no place to move to if I had.

The muzzle of that pistol looked bigger and bigger. Then deliberately he shifted his aim about six inches and fired.

The muzzle flowered with flame, the slug smashed into the earth beside my head. He re-cocked his pistol, took dead aim, holding on a spot right between my eyes, and then again he shifted his aim and fired. The concussion was terrific, but when I opened my eyes he was sitting there looking down at me from those utterly cold gray eyes. Coolly, he blew the smoke from the muzzle of his gun and, turning his horse, rode off after the others.

The drum of his horse's hoofs faded, but I could

not move. I lay staring up at the low gray clouds that now covered even that far-off place where the sun had gone down, but at last something stirred inside me, some strange, crying need to struggle back, to survive. So I rolled over on my face.

My body ached with the dull throb of bruised and battered muscle and bone. Yet somehow I got my hands under me and pushed myself up to my knees. One eye was closed, the other a mere slit, and when I lifted my fumbling, bloody hands to my face they recoiled in horror. It was swollen out of shape and torn into what must be an awful mask.

Grasping the edge of the wallow, I pulled myself up. But my legs gave way and I fell, my chin hitting the ground so heavily that a thousand new pains started in my skull. After a minute I tried again, this time digging my fingers into the half-frozen soil and pulling myself up out of the wallow.

It took all the strength I had, and I lay there on the ground. Far off I seemed to hear shooting. . . . So then it was no use—they had caught up with my friends and were murdering them.

The cold of the earth seeped into my bones, and I shook with a chill. One hand reached out and grasped a tuft of grass and pulled my body toward it.

A drop of blood fell from my face and made a bright crimson spot on my sleeve. I stared at it dully for a moment, then I got my hands under me and began to crawl forward. This time I must have crawled several feet before I collapsed again, and then I passed out from weakness.

I woke in the night to cold and a raging thirst. Reaching out, I got a handful of half-frozen snow and thrust it at my mouth. I felt the tearing of partly closed cuts, and my jaw creaked with pain at the effort to open my mouth, but some of the snow got through. It melted, and a slow, delicious trickle started down my throat.

My body ached, but again I got to my knees and started forward. After a few minutes I came abreast of a rock and, catching hold of it, pulled myself up, clinging to it until my legs stopped trembling.

Staggering, I started forward. Somehow I would get to Miles City, and when I got there I would find Roman Bohlen. Somehow, some way, I would find him.

It was that thought which saved me, which drove me on through a terrible, agony-filled night, when I staggered, fell, climbed up, and fell again. Twice I spilled over creek banks to the ice below but each time I managed to get up, and struggled on.

The coming of a sickly gray dawn found me still walking and falling, still getting up again. My hands were bloody, my body ached, every step wrenched a groan from me, but I kept on. Somewhere up ahead was whatever remained of my friends, for the shots I had heard could only have meant that Bohlen and his outfit had closed in around them.

There is something to be said for hatred under such circumstances. Certainly, without it I could never have gotten myself off the ground, not as much as ten feet from where I started.

The distance was measured at first in feet, but finally I came to measuring it merely in paces. To look ahead, to try to imagine covering the bitter miles would have been impossible. If I could manage just the next step, I was satisfied.

One of my hands—I had no memory of this—had been stomped on. It was lacerated and terribly swollen, but the fingers could move, though with so much pain that I had no intention of trying to use that hand.

One or more of my ribs might be broken . . . they felt like it. I was cut, bruised, and battered, and that, coupled with the exhaustion of the days before, had left me with almighty little to travel on but nerve.

And hatred.

I wanted most of all to kill Roman Bohlen.

Sometimes I was out of my head. Sometimes the horizon seemed to dip and waver around me. Walking and falling, I doubt if I made a mile that first day.

Toward nightfall something moved off to my right. Later, I glimpsed it again.

It was a wolf. No coyote, but a big old gray lobo, and he was stalking me.

They'd taken my guns and my knife, and I couldn't even find anything for a club. I had no defense against him.

A wolf will not tackle a man. I'd been told that since I was a youngster, and I believed it . . . up to a point.

That old lobo out there knew I was all in. He knew his time would come; and a wolf, like a buzzard, has a vast patience at such times. Sometimes I think only man is in a rush about things. Most wild animals, with no sense of time to speak of, they can wait. They know how to wait.

He might get me tonight. It might be tomorrow or tomorrow night—he wasn't in a rush about it.

Once, when I fell down, I lay for several minutes without moving. I seemed only half conscious. When I moved to get up, there was the wolf, sitting there, not fifty yards away, tongue lolling out, watching me.

CHAPTER 17

HE MADE ME mad, sitting there, just waiting for me to give up, and so damned sure he was going to have me when I couldn't go any further. So I got up and started on, and I had a sort of notion that I might move briskly enough to persuade him the wait would be too long. But I saw at once that he wasn't being fooled. Nevertheless I kept going. Several times I stopped for a handful of snow, but I kept on going until it was too dark to make out landmarks, and with no stars to be seen, I was afraid to travel on for fear of going out of my way in the wrong direction.

About that time I struck my first streak of pay dirt. It wasn't much—just a thick clump of willow and chokecherry with a couple of cottonwoods on the bank of a small frozen stream, but the thing was, there was a lot of debris around, so I searched my pockets again and found a couple of matches. On the under side of an old dead tree I found some bark which I frayed in my fingers. I broke off some tiny twigs and found some dry moss, and then struck my match. The first one took flame, and soon I had a good fire going.

They'd left me for dead, and by this time were far away, so I had no worry about having a fire, and it was something badly needed, both for warmth and for bracing up my morale, or whatever they call it.

No searching of my pockets yielded anything to eat; not a crumb could I find. But the warmth of the fire was making me sleepy, and I hovered close to it.

And then I heard a horse walking.

It was close on to midnight now, and I had been dozing and waking, feeding the fire and dozing again. The clouds had broken a little, and I could see the stars. There was no use my trying to run, but I did reach over and lay my hand on a good-sized club I'd found while gathering fuel.

The horse walked steadily toward me, hesitated, and then came on, more slowly, stopping from time to time.

I stood up. If that horse had a rider it wasn't acting like it; and if rider there was, he was either dead or helpless.

The horse stopped just outside the rim of the firelight. It was a saddled, bridled horse, and it was looking toward me, ears pricked. When I stepped away from the glare of the fire I saw it was Ann's horse, one of those fine Morgans Philo had shipped west to breed.

He was off-color, a blue roan, but a fine, beautifully built horse, one of the best Farley had. He called him Blue Boy.

"Hello, Boy," I said gently. "Where's Ann?"

The horse came another tentative step forward and stood uncertainly, rolling his eyes at me and spreading his nostrils. So I walked over to him, moving very slowly. He was probably drawn to the fire because it promised what he had become accustomed to, the companionship of man. And that horse meant life itself to me.

"Where's Ann, Boy?" I said again, and kept on talking quietly to him. "I'm glad you showed up. Maybe we can go back there and see what happened. Just you and me. What d'you say?"

For an instant, as I neared him, I was afraid he would shy away. But he stood fast, and then, as I put a hand on his neck, he turned his head and stretched his nose at me, and I gathered up the reins.

My heart was pounding enough to jump out of my chest from the fear I'd had that the horse might jerk away and trot off. For if once he started going, I might have chased him halfway to Miles City and never got that close again. So now I led him over to the fire and tied him carefully while I checked the saddlebags.

In the first bag I found several cartridges, there was no gun in the saddle scabbard, but a brush, comb, and some other trifles. In the other bag—I could hardly believe my luck—there was a sandwich of two thick slices of bread and a wedge of beef. It was a couple of days old, but when I started to eat it I savored every bite, taking as much time chewing as I possibly could.

It is a mistake to think that a hungry man bolts his food. He does nothing of the kind. His stomach has shrunk; and anyway, he wants to chew, to taste, to savor every bite. He eats slowly, and that first time after he's been a long time hungry, he can eat very little. This time I hadn't been hungry really long, but it had been too long.

When I had eaten the sandwich I rustled around and found a small patch of snow-free grass and led the horse to it. He ate so eagerly that I knew he had found mighty little grazing.

Right then was when I wanted to start for Miles City, but I knew that first I had to back-track that horse and find out what had happened to the Farleys and Eddie. Tired as I was, I slept little, waiting for morning to come so I could see to pick up Blue Boy's trail.

It was mid-morning when I found them in a small patch of wooded hills half surrounded by Ash and Haddow creeks. They were in a narrow ravine where a branch of Ash Creek flowed down out of the hills. It was a lonely, out-of-the-way place and not bad for defense, only from the way the ground was torn up the Bohlen men must have come on them as a complete surprise.

There was a dead horse on the ground, and further over, a dead man. It was a man named Cruickshank, I think—I'd seen him around. He had been shot in the chest, killed instantly.

At first I saw no other bodies, and my hopes began to rise. Maybe they had gotten away, maybe . . . And then I saw the torn earth at the creek's edge. It was a place where somebody without tools had tried breaking off the earth with sticks and tumbling it down to cover up what lay below.

Running my horse up there, I jumped off, tying the horse to make doubly sure of him, and then I went over the bank, my pulse jumping like a crazy man's.

The three bodies lay together, only half covered, so they must have tried to cover them at night, maybe figuring on coming back later to finish the job.

Philo was dead, shot to doll rags. Eddie had a bullet in his leg, and when I pulled him from under the dirt, I saw he had taken two more through the chest. His shirt had pulled up, and for the first time I saw the earlier wound in the side from which he'd lost blood. He had told me it was nothing, but now I could see the bullet had torn a frightful gash in his side, and he must have been almost bled dry. He had stuffed the wound with the tail of his shirt and belted it in place with an extra belt, but it had obviously begun to infect almost from the start.

Purposely, I'd hesitated to look at Ann, for I didn't want to admit to myself that she was dead.

She was the furthest from me, and when I did turn to look, I got the shock of my life. There were faint furrows behind her toes!

She had not been dead when she was thrown into the gully, and after they had tumbled dirt upon her, she had pulled herself free of it.

Dropping beside her, I turned her over, and when I did this, her mouth fell open and I saw her tongue move.

I had no canteen or cup, but I grabbed up a busted rifle and smashed the ice with the butt. Then dipping a spare handkerchief I'd found with her things in the saddlebag, I took it to her and squeezed a few drops into her mouth.

Then I stretched her out on my bloody sheepskin

coat. She'd been shot through the shoulder, and her clothing was soaked with blood. Only the cold had saved her, as it had Shorty, by coagulating the blood to stop the bleeding. It looked as if she had a broken leg, too, and she must be half frozen.

Quickly I dragged some sticks into a pile near her, scrounged for some dried leaves, then pulled out my one match and tried to strike it. It broke off short.

I went through her pockets frantically. No matches. There were none in Eddie's pockets, either, and most of the dirt from the bank lay over the lower half of Philo's body, covering it up to his waist. Rather than take the time to uncover him and risk the possible cave-in that might follow, I scrambled back up the bank and ran to the body of Cruickshank.

In his shirt pocket was an old brass cartridge shell with several matches, and a packet of tobacco, with papers.

Using the papers as tinder, I struck a light and had me a fire. When it was going well, I stretched it out to parallel her body, with the wind blowing the flames away from her. Then I went to the dead horse.

It was Philo's own horse, and in the saddlebags was what remained of his gear, for we'd abandoned some of it when we left the sled. In that pocket was a small packet of tea.

Digging around in the dirt and debris that had

been pushed down or thrown over the edge, I found a cup and the battered coffeepot we had been using. Obviously Bohlen's men had been in a big hurry to get away, for they had just dumped everything over, bodies and gear, and then had hurried off, probably wanting to arrive in Miles City and be seen there.

At this time of year, in that remote place, there was small chance of any discovery. It was off the trails, and in a place where I doubted anyone had been in years.

Ann's leg was broken, so, as carefully as I could, I put splints on it and tied them up with strips cut from a bridle with Cruickshank's knife. It was just a jack-knife, the kind we used to call a toad-stabber back in school when I was a kid. But Cruickshank had kept it good and sharp, for which I owed him thanks.

The water had just started to boil in the bent-up old pot when Ann opened her eyes. There was mud and blood in her hair and her clothes were badly torn, her face was drawn and so white she looked like a corpse.

"You lie quiet," I said before she could speak. "You've been shot and you've got a broken leg."

"I know," she said faintly.

She said nothing at all about the others, so I think she knew very well they were dead, but she kept looking at my face with such a shocked expression that I put my hand up to it, and for the first time in hours I remembered what they had done to me.

"Well," I said, "I was never what you'd call a handsome man, anyway. Nobody will be surprised."

What tea there was I dumped into the pot, and set it to one side to steep a mite. Then I rinsed out the cup in the creek, heated it over the fire to take the chill off so's it wouldn't ruin the effect of the hot tea, and then I filled the cup and held it for her to drink.

While she worked on the tea, I told her about being left for dead, being found by her horse, evidently attracted by my fire, and coming on to hunt for her.

"My guess is that Bohlen and his men will ride around and come into Miles City from the north or east. They'll give out they were off in that direction, toward the Badlands. They'll come out here the first chance they get to bury what's left, but first they'll get everybody used to the idea that they're in town.

"The folks in Miles City are good people. Some of them, like Stuart, are sympathetic to the vigilante way as long as it's handled with care, but nobody would have wanted anything like this to happen. My feeling is that when this story gets out, Bohlen is through. They'll run him out of the country . . . or I will."

"Barney, you can't. You're all I have left."

"I've got it to do."

"You can't, Barney. If I lost you—"

She didn't know what she was saying. "You've got a brother back in England, a fine home. You've got everything back there."

"I've nothing back there, nothing at all. I was always closest to Philo, and he knew how I felt. I always envied him his Army career in India, and I wanted to come with him when he first came here."

Dragging up a dead branch, I broke off twigs and thrust them into the flames. "You got nerve enough to try riding thirty miles?" I asked her.

"Yes."

She had it, too.

"They'll never let us get into town if they see me coming," I said. "I've got to have a gun."

She turned her head suddenly, reaching out the cup to me. "Is there more?"

Then she went on. "Back about a mile, where the creek comes down from the west, Eddie shot a man. He fell from his horse, and when he was hit I saw him throw his rifle wide. It may not have been found."

It was nearly noon now, and with two of us riding one horse we weren't going to make it to Miles City before the next day. The best thing would be to come in after dark so I could get Ann to a doctor before anybody saw me. The thing I had to do now was to get that gun.

She made me drink a cup of the tea before I left,

and it surely did me good. I'd never thought much of tea as a man's drink, although Philo had tried to convince me it was a good thing when a man was cold or suffering from shock. So they'd found it, he said, in the British Army, and in mountain climbing.

Feeling the way I did, that was a long hike, and I was glad to stop when I got there. I'd left our horse with Ann. That horse was our life, and he had been badly used during the past few days, and I wanted to take him no step that wasn't toward Miles City and safety.

Finding the rifle was no trick. When I saw the tracks and found where the horse had thrown its rider, I scouted out in an arc from the body and found it, half buried in snow but in good working condition.

What had become of the horse? I looked around, but there was no luck.

So I started back, but I was feeling better. In the pockets of the dead man I had found six more cartridges, and there were six in the rifle. I could do a lot with twelve shots. Especially if I could get my man in the street.

Roman Bohlen had tackled the wrong outfit. With his hired killers and his tough hands he had started out to kill three men and a girl. He'd had nine men in all, and four of them were dead —four of them, and two of us.

But the two men he had killed were good men,

and Eddie Holt had been my partner. It would be a long time before I'd run into another like Eddie.

Right now I wanted most to get Ann in a doctor's hands, and then I only wanted one thing.

I wanted to look down that rifle barrel at Roman Bohlen—just once.

CHAPTER 18

MILES CITY WASN'T just a cowtown, for Fort Keogh was close by with around a thousand men—soldiers and civilian employees. Then the Diamond R bull-whackers numbered quite a few, and when not slugging it out in some street brawl with the swaddies, as they called the soldiers from Fort Keogh, they could be counted on to voice opinions that carried weight in any gathering. And I was counting on them, if it came to that.

If we could ride into town after nightfall, I could take Ann to the Inter-Ocean Hotel—the one they now were calling the Macqueen House. The hotel was right on the road into town, and with a little luck I could get Ann into it and safe before the Bohlen crowd even knew we were alive.

We started off that night, and rode about ten miles before we settled down for the night. I'd taken the blanket off the dead horse, so we had that, and there was my sheepskin coat.

Before daybreak we rode for some distance, and

then after a short rest we went on a little further, keeping to low ground. By late afternoon we were within a few miles of town.

We waited in a creek bed near the Tongue River for the sun to go down. Ann's face was so white it scared me. The death of Eddie and her brother, on top of everything else, had been about all she could stand.

"Ann," I said to her, and I took her by the arms, "it's just a bit longer. We'll ride into town, and you'll be safe in the Macqueen House. You've friends there."

Her eyes were hollow with exhaustion, but there was fire in them still as she faced me. "What about you? What will you do?"

"What remains to be done," I said. "I've got to see the sheriff and tell him about Philo and Eddie. They'll send a buckboard out for them."

"And then?"

She was a hard one to fool, and it wasn't in me to lie overmuch, so I just shrugged and said, "I guess the rest of it is up to the sheriff," and I turned away.

Well, she wasn't long from England, and over there they have respect for the law, and let the law take its course, as should be done everywhere. Only here in the West there sometimes wasn't much law, and there were some things the law and other folks preferred a man settle for himself. At any rate, I intended to settle what lay between myself and Roman Bohlen.

As we came down the road into town, I heard a train whistle, a lonesome, far-off sound that always made me want to go to all the places I'd never been. There for a moment I felt the pull of it—but first things first. I had an idea that when Ann was safe among her own kind, then it would be time for me to do what had to be done, and then I would grab myself an armful of boxcars and leave out of there.

It was late when we finally came up to the Macqueen House. I got down and helped Ann from the saddle.

When we went through the door the first person we ran into was Verna Elwin. She was the wife of an Englishman visiting up on the Musselshell, and an old friend of Ann's, so I left her with her. But Ann turned at the door. "Barney . . . come to see me. Come tomorrow."

"Sure," I said. "I'll do just that."

And all the while I was sure it was the last time I'd ever see her. A girl like her, under the conditions we'd been living under, she might say or even believe unaccountable things. But when she had rested a couple of days, the last person she would want to see would be me, a broken-down cowhand.

And I had a thing to do.

Outside, I mounted and rode down to the livery stable and left the horse to be cared for. Then I taken my rifle and faced up the street.

Main Street wasn't much when it came to that, just those false-fronted frame buildings, some of them with rough-cut boards outside the original logs. There were lights up there, and a few people moving along the street.

I pulled my hat brim down and walked up the street, the rifle in the hollow of my arm, and went along to Charley Brown's.

When I pushed open the door, the first person I laid eyes on was Roman Bohlen.

He stiffened up as if he was shot, but I give him credit. He thought faster and moved faster than me.

"Sheriff!" he called out to the man at the bar. "Arrest that man! He and that nigger partner of his murdered the Farleys. Murdered them and shot up my men when we tried to take them!"

It was the last thing I expected, and it caught me flat-footed. I yelled back at him, "That's a damn lie, an' you know it! You—"

"Take him, sheriff, before he shoots somebody else!"

And the sheriff stepped back from the bar and said, "Give me the rifle, Pronto. Come on, now. Give it to me."

"Sheriff, he's lyin'! He and those hands of his, they murdered Farley for a rustler. They killed Eddie Holt, my partner, and—"

"You give me the gun," the sheriff said, "and we'll talk about it."

There were men in that room whom I counted

as friends, but two of Bohlen's men were standing by the door, their hands on their guns. If shooting started, innocent folks would die. So I handed over my gun.

WHEN I FELL on the bunk in the jail I never even had time to think or to worry, I just naturally passed out. Fact was, by the time I got to the jailhouse I was walking in a daze. The whole thing was out of my hands, and everything inside me just seemed to let go. I'd been running afoot, fighting, going hungry, riding it seemed forever, and when I fell down on that bunk I never even hauled off my boots.

Next thing I knew somebody was shaking me. "You going to sleep forever? Man here to see you."

Rolling over, I sat up, blinking. It was daylight, looked to be noon or after. Standing at the bars was Butch Hogan.

"Pike," he said, "no matter what they say, I don't believe it. You'd never murder anybody."

Looking past him, I could see the sheriff standing there with Bill Justin and another man. When they saw me looking at them, they turned their backs on me.

"They're saying you killed Farley and his sister. Murdered them," Hogan said.

"That's a damn lie! It was Bohlen."

Butch Hogan, who wasn't much on the talk, gave me the story as he'd heard it. Roman Bohlen had come into town and had spread the story that after Justin had fired me for rustling I'd gone hog-wild. That I'd shot and killed Farley, and had ambushed them in company with Eddie Holt.

Nobody knew anything about Holt, and I had a bad reputation for fighting, though I was a hard-working hand. And there were plenty to recall the bad things about me and forget the good. Bohlen, after all, was an established rancher, a man with some standing, and I was just a cowhand who might drift on out of the country.

Farley's friends were as sore as I'd thought they would be, only they believed I was the killer and it was me they were sore at. Some of the toughs around town were talking a lynching party. And the funny thing was that the only one standing by me was a man I'd fought twice on mighty little provocation.

Nobody had mentioned Ann Farley, and I wasn't about to. When she heard of all this she'd come forward. Tired as she was, she was likely still asleep, and no use to have her waked up. Besides, jail was as good a place to sleep as any, and Bohlen could wait.

"You're in real trouble," Hogan said to me. "You'd better get you a lawyer."

"With what?"

"Well, me an' the boys could probably—"

"Don't worry your head about it. I ain't worried. Roman Bohlen did it, and—"

196

"That ain't going to he'p none," Hogan insisted. "You can't lay it on him." He glanced right and left. "You want to bust out of here, the boys an' me will he'p you."

"Forget it."

"Ain't there anything I can do?"

"Come to think of it, there is. If you see Jim Fargo around, you tell him I want to see him."

After Hogan had gone I tried to go back to sleep, but I couldn't. The way the sheriff and those others had turned their backs on me stayed in my mind. Of a sudden, my eyes opened wide. They really believed all that! They believed that I had murdered the Farleys. . . .

But Ann was still alive!

Didn't they know *that?* The answer was obvious: they did not know it or they wouldn't be accusing me of it. What was more, Roman Bohlen didn't know Ann was alive, either.

What would he do when he found out? The answer to that was simple. She'd have to be stopped from talking. She would have to be killed.

But why hadn't she told them the truth of what had happened out there?

Thinking back over my few words with Hogan, I realized that while he believed me, at least in part, he didn't think I had a chance or he wouldn't be offering to help me break out. For the first time I was scared.

Suddenly I wished Ann was here. I surely didn't

want to hang, and I didn't want Bohlen to go scot-free.

Nobody else came near me. The jailer, a man I'd often bought drinks for and talked with, brought me my meals, but he didn't say a word. The dislike in his manner was mighty apparent, and it began to look as if I didn't have a friend anywhere.

During the next couple of days, I overheard talk. They said I'd been stealing from Justin all the time, and from Bohlen, that I had always been a trouble-maker and was never any good.

Hogan came back to see me and told me they'd tried to get a lawyer for me, but not one would touch the case.

"Look," I said, "go out to the Macqueen House and ask Ann Farley to come and see me."

Hogan looked at me as if I'd gone crazy. "What are you talkin' about? Ann Farley's dead."

"No, she isn't," I said. "She rode in with me that night. I left her at the Macqueen House with Verna Elwin."

He looked at me uneasily, and I could see he was doubting me, only it was my sanity he was doubting.

"I'll go ask," he said reluctantly, and then he added, "Jim Fargo's not in town. He's been appointed a Deputy U.S. Marshal, and he's workin' on some rustling down along the Wyoming border—some new outfit. They came in out of nowhere and drove off most of Justin's stock and some of Bohlen's, to say nothing of almost everything in the Badlands."

Well, that had to be an exaggeration, but they must have done plenty to cause all that talk.

It was the next morning before Hogan came in again. He looked worried, and his eyes searched my face—he seemed to be looking for something there, maybe some sign that I was going off my head.

"She ain't there," he said, "and they never saw her."

That made the bottom drop out of everything. I stood there, clutching the bars. "Butch," I said, "damn it, they've got me. If you can't find Ann Farley, and if she won't come forward, Bohlen's going to swear me right into a hangman's noose."

Hogan stood there uneasily, and I could see that not even he believed me any longer.

"I got to go," he said. "I'm goin' out with a freight outfit. Goin' down to Cheyenne."

My shoulders sagged. "Luck," I said, "and thanks, Butch. Looks like you're the only friend I've got."

He sort of relented then. "No, I ain't. Charley Brown still swears he don't believe it. In fact, he nearly got into a shooting with one of Bohlen's men over it."

Hogan paused as he turned away from the door. "One thing you were right about," he commented. "Mrs. Elwin was at the hotel that night.

Only she left and drove out to that ranch where she's stayin'."

For a moment that gave me a bit of hope. Then maybe Ann wasn't just ignoring me. Maybe she had gone off to the ranch with the Elwins to recover, and didn't even know what was happening. Suddenly I was sure that was what had happened. Verna Elwin was a nice woman, but she was also a bossy, managing type, and Ann would have been in no state to argue with her. It would be just like Mrs. Elwin, seeing the shape Ann was in, to cart her off to give her a rest. From what I knew of the Elwins, though they were nice folks, they were stand-offish. Out on that ranch they might not be seeing many people and they might not know what was going on at all.

I'd be lying if I didn't admit I was scared. And all the time, Bohlen was out there, walking the streets and trying with every word to be sure that I'd hang.

On the fourth morning the jailer showed up with Doc Finerty from Fort Keogh. The Doc was a man I'd seen around town but I didn't know him. It seems the local doctor was out of town, so they'd asked Doc Finerty to have a look at me.

Or had he decided himself on coming? I never did know the straight of that.

He checked the cuts on my face, which were several shades of blue and yellow and still swollen. "You'll carry a couple of scars," he said.

"From the way they talk, I'll not carry them long."

"Well, you did it, didn't you?"

"Like hell!" I said.

He had me take off my shirt. As he checked me over he asked questions and talked all around it until he got me to tell the whole story. He didn't make any comment while I talked, just taping up my ribs and putting some medicine on my torn hand, which was still in bad shape.

"They ever bring the bodies in?" I asked. "Ann would be mighty upset if she knew her brother's body was lying out for the wolves, like that."

"Wolves didn't touch them, Pike," Finerty said. "I examined the bodies when they were brought in."

"I wish we'd had you out there," I said. "Farley was dead game. He had a rough ride on that sled, and then on horseback after. Funny thing, he seemed to be getting better. If it hadn't been for them killing him, I think he'd have recovered."

Finerty made no comment at that; he just rolled the cigar in his mouth and closed his bag. Then he said, "That's the first time I've heard of a sled. Farley was wounded then?"

"Roman Bohlen," I said, "started out with a bunch of his own private vigilantes. To him Philo Farley was just another nester, and to him all nesters are rustlers. He didn't know a damned thing about Farley's background, and cared less.

"Farley told me that Bohlen shot him when he, Farley, was unarmed, that Bohlen would have hung him if he hadn't escaped. Then I helped them. We built a sled because Farley was in no shape to ride."

"What happened to the sled?"

I told him about the ambush on the pass in the Cook Mountains, and how we abandoned the sled.

"You know," Finerty said, "they are accusing you of killing Johnny Ward too."

Well, why not? I was being accused of everything else. Why not throw all the crimes in a basket and hang me for the lot?

"Did Bohlen do that?" Finerty asked. He studied me with those steely gray eyes of his and chewed on his cigar, waiting for my answer.

"Funny thing, about that. I never have figured it out." I explained about the leather-shod hoofs, and even about finding those same tracks near Farley's place.

"One time there I thought it might be that strange woman, but her mule didn't wear leather shoes—though he did have mighty small feet."

"What woman was that?"

So I told him about the woman I'd seen, and what Ann had told me about her spilling a pot of beans at Farley's place when she saw Ann there.

"This woman—what did she look like?"

"A big woman, big frame anyway, and kind of stupid-looking. Dressed in a man's rough cast-off clothes—clothes for a much bigger person than she was. I'll admit she worried me some, spooking around like that."

"Pike, when did you first come into this country?"

"Me? Around '74, I guess, but I didn't stay long. I was back in '79, and a couple of times after that. Those times when I came back I worked around over the country."

"You weren't here when Clyde Orum was around, were you?"

"Hell, the way I hear it, not even Miles City was here."

Doc Finerty took a cigar from his pocket and handed it to me. "Clyde had quite a family. I was reared over west of here, Pike, over south of Butte, near Virginia City. I knew the Orums."

"Yeah?"

"Clyde Orum had a sister, much younger than he was, and she worshiped the ground he walked on. I don't think she was quite right mentally."

"What I hear," I said, "Clyde was kind of an odd one himself."

"Do you see what I'm getting at, Pike? If that was Lottie Orum out there, she would have had reason to kill Johnny Ward. He was in the posse that rounded up Clyde, and he testified in court against him."

"What about Shorty Cones?"

Finerty shrugged. "I don't know about that,

although she might have had a reason there too."

"Doc, can you get word up to the Elwins? I mean, no matter what anybody says, Ann Farley is still alive. That Orum woman now, her seeing Ann there like that, she probably thought Ann was Farley's woman, and I think the Orum woman was sweet on Farley her ownself."

"So?"

"So she might try to kill Ann. Thing is, not one of those folks she killed was expecting it."

After Finerty had gone I lay back on my bunk and stared up at the ceiling. No matter whether he had said anything that helped, I surely did feel better. I felt a lot better. Now if I could only get out of here.

Rubbing out the cigar, I laid it on the window sill for future use. My hand felt better already. Doc had told me it should be soaked twice a day in hot water and Epsom salts. I'd heard him tell the jailer that.

CHAPTER 19

A BOUT AN HOUR after Doc Finerty left, the jailer came with a cup of coffee, which he passed through the bars.

"Doc thinks you got a bad deal," he said.

"He's got company," I said.

When darkness came again I went to the window and got my cigar. I lit up and smoked a couple of minutes, then I rubbed out the cigar again, went to my bunk, and went to sleep.

About midnight I suddenly woke up, startled out of a sound sleep by a lot of banging around. The cell next to mine was opened and a man was shoved in, the door closed, and the jailer went away.

For a while there was silence, but when I turned over the bunk creaked and a voice said, "Who's in there?"

"It's me," I said, "Pike. What did they get you for?"

"Hell, what d'you think? Rustling. I stole all the damn cows in the country, and then that Jim Fargo showed up. Won't do him no good. I got those cows clean out of the country, and when this trial is over and I go free, I've got me a stake."

I knew the voice, knew the familiar sound of the bragging. It was Van Bokkelen, and I might have guessed he had moved into rustling. It was about the only big crooked operation around, and just the sort of thing he would seek out.

"You think you'll go clear?" I asked.

He laughed. "Why, you damn fool, this country has the best judges that money can buy, and believe me, they can be bought. If this case ever comes to trial, I'll go free. I'll have me a good lawyer, and I'll prove it was all a mistake.

"Anyway, they could only get me for rustling, and I could do the years I'd get for that standing on my head."

"You talk a good show."

"I'm better off than you," he said contemptuously. "At least, I'm in here for something I did."

He had me there, so I turned over and tried to go to sleep again.

But after maybe half an hour had passed and I was still lying there thinking, he said, "Hell, I got a good notion to bust out. You want to try it?"

"No."

"The hell with you!"

That ended our conversation.

MY HAND WAS getting better, but it needed to, with what I had planned for it.

At noon on my sixth day in jail the door from the office opened suddenly and Jim Fargo appeared. He had the keys in his hand, and he unlocked the door of my cell. "Come on out, Pike," he said. "You don't belong in there."

"Am I free?"

"No, there's a preliminary hearing this morning. That's where we're going now."

"Will Roman Bohlen be there?"

"He had better be."

The room was crowded when Fargo walked me to the front of the room, and I could hear the muttering as I passed. Butch Hogan and Charley Brown were there, and at the back of the room there was a row of soldiers wearing side arms.

Roman Bohlen and his outfit were there, and

Red Hardeman was with them. When they brought me in Bohlen shot an ugly look at Hardeman, but the gunman never flickered his eyelids.

Bohlen testified, telling how I'd stolen stock from Justin and himself, how I'd been fired, and how I'd gone crazy and killed the Farleys, then attacked his outfit when Eddie Holt was killed by them.

"The Farleys were both killed?" the judge asked.

"Both of them. I saw her body, too. I don't know what he did with it."

At that moment the door opened and Ann walked in on crutches. She was pale, but she looked better than when I'd last seen her, and she walked right up to me and held out her hand.

"I am very sorry, Barney," she said, "but I've been ill. I didn't know."

She looked wonderful to me. "Forget it," I said.

All the while there was a hush in the room, everybody looking at Roman Bohlen. His mouth opened and closed a couple of times, and once he moved as if to rise, but those soldiers were all standing now, right across the back of the room, and he stayed where he was.

Ann took the stand and told her story simply and directly. Then she took from her purse a sheet of folded paper. "Your honor, this was written before my brother died. Surely, if Mr. Pike had been involved in any way at all, my brother would not have done this."

The judge glanced at it. "I know that signature," he said.

Then Doc Finerty testified that he became doubtful of Bohlen's story when he examined the wounds on the dead men. They didn't fit with the circumstances of Bohlen's story, for both Farley and Holt had wounds older than the recital of events given by Bohlen.

Then the judge asked me to identify the men with Bohlen, and I did so, until I came to Red Hardeman. He was looking at me out of those steely eyes and showed no emotion whatsoever.

"Your honor," I said, "I never saw this man in that bunch—he wasn't among them. Anyway, I know this man, and he wouldn't be involved in anything of the kind. There's been a mistake."

Roman Bohlen's face was ugly. "By the—"

"Shut up!" Fargo snapped. Then he said to the sheriff, "These men are in your custody. Leave Hardeman here. I want to speak to him."

Ann waited at the back of the room. Jim Fargo, Red Hardeman, and me, we stood together by ourselves.

"Red," Fargo said, "you know and I know that you were there. What Pike did that for, I don't know; but if he did it he had a good reason. Do you know anybody in Texas?"

"I got kin there."

"Have you got a fast horse?"

"I have."

"Then go visit your kin . . . and stay out of Montana."

Ann and me, we walked back up the street together, and I was some embarrassed to see the way some of those no-account cowhands stared at us, to say nothing about those bull-whackers from the Diamond R.

"That was Philo's will that I gave to the judge. He left his stock to you, all his cattle and his horses."

"Why me?"

"Why not? You helped us, when nobody else would. Just you and that Negro."

"He was a good man, Eddie was." I looked down at my hand and doubled my fist. "He taught me to fight."

"Philo had almost three hundred head of fine beef cattle and at least fifty horses. We could start a ranch."

Well, I didn't know what to say. This was what I'd been dreaming of, but dreams are nothing to take seriously. Or maybe they are. . . . I only know that here it was, more chance than a tough-hided cowhand deserved.

"If you mean it," I said, "I'll try to make it so you won't be sorry later."

"Philo said you'd never marry me unless you had something of your own, and he said you'd earned it during all that terrible trip across country."

"I'd be a fool to argue," I said.

209

We stopped near the steps of the hotel and I didn't know what to say. It was the first time I'd ever been engaged to a girl, and the first time I'd been in love since I was fourteen, and then the girl never knew it. I stood there, wanting to kiss her, thinking I should, and feeling like a damned fool. And then she reached up and kissed me very gently on the lips and went inside, and I turned around quick, expecting somebody to laugh.

There were a few cowhands in sight, and a couple of bull-whackers, but all of them were very busy at whatever they were doing, which wasn't much. So I walked over to Charley Brown's, my feet scarcely touching the ground.

Some of the boys were there and I bought a drink, and looked off into a fine, friendly world, suddenly richer and better off than I'd ever expected to be, and engaged to an Irish girl who would soon be my wife.

Looking at myself in the mirror, my face still ugly from the beating I'd taken from Bohlen, I couldn't figure what she saw in me. But a man's life is much in his own hands, and what I was did not have to be the measure of what I would be. Sure, I wasn't brilliant, but I've seen a few of all kinds, and in the long drive give me a man who is persistent rather than brilliant. Too often the brilliant ones are flashes in the pan, no more.

I finished my drink and stepped out on the walk and stood there, breathing in that good Montana air and figuring I had the world laid out before me like a banquet.

Sure . . . it would take a lot of work. Philo had left me whatever he had here in Montana, and though it wasn't such a lot as wealth goes, it was a good start, and with my know-how and savvy I should make a go of it.

First things first. I must walk down to the livery stable and check on that horse of Ann's. He'd been badly beat when I took him in, and while they took good care of horses, I'd better have a look.

The horse turned his head and nickered when I came up to the stall and spoke to him. I expect he was lonesome, for once a horse becomes addicted to people he likes them about, and he likes people he knows. So I stood there, telling him about Ann and me, and what he could look forward to in that ranch over against the Big Horns. Then I slapped him on the hip and stepped out of the stall, and looked right into a gun.

Van Bokkelen was holding it, and he was looking across that gun and grinning at me. Roman Bohlen was right there beside him.

I wasn't wearing a gun and it wouldn't have done me any good if I had been.

"You wouldn't bust out with me," Van Bokkelen said, "so I brought Bohlen along."

"I'm going to kill him," Bohlen said, "with my bare hands."

Deliberately, Van Bokkelen holstered his gun.

"You do what you are of a mind to," he said. "I'll saddle the horses."

Roman Bohlen was big, and he was fast and mean. He had whipped Hogan, who had whipped me twice. He stood between me and the door as if he thought I would try to get away. The only way I was going out of here was through him or over him.

He didn't say a word, he just cut loose and swung, and I hit him in the belly with my right fist. The blow was perfectly timed and it caught him coming in, just like Eddie had showed me. It stopped him dead in his tracks, leaving him wide open for the left I smashed into his mouth.

That was my sore hand, and it hurt, but it also plastered Bohlen's mouth. And then he went berserk.

He came at me swinging and all I could do was slip inside of one punch and grab hold with both hands. He backheeled me, but when we hit ground I jerked my knee up, and while it didn't hurt him it threw him on over me and I whirled around and slid from under.

We both came up punching. Over the saddle he was cinching on a horse, Van Bokkelen was watching, unconcerned as though he was at the ringside of a fight.

After those first two good punches I must have got hit a dozen times, but they were mostly mauling, bruising punches that battered at my shoulders and chest without doing me much harm. The one or two that did get through shook me to my heels.

My face was already sore, and his punches there really hurt. But I got in another good smash to the body.

He knocked me down twice, but both times I got out of the way before he could kick me, and then we tied into each other again, and he threw me with a rolling hip-lock. I dove into his knees and he came down half on top of me, and I squirmed from under and was the first man on his feet. When he was halfway up I caught him on the nose with a full swing, and the blood gushed.

He charged at me and I stood my ground, swinging in with both hands. He hurt me with a right hand, and then tried it again, but that time I hit him with another right to the body, then a left and another right to the same place. He backed up, a sick look on his face, and I walked into him, suddenly confident that I could take him.

All the time I could hear Eddie's words. "Make him miss, then hit him. He'll be a head-hunter, always punching for the face and jaw, so make him miss and hit him where he lives. No matter how tough they are, that'll bring 'em down."

I feinted, and when he lunged at me I belted him with an uppercut in the wind. He gasped and his jaw fell slack, and I moved on into him.

"Looks like you need some help," Van Bokkelen

213

said then, and he stepped in, balancing that six-shooter for a chop at my neck. "You ain't doing so good, Roman."

Bohlen, getting a moment's breath, lifted a hand to wipe the blood off his mouth, and I threw the works into a right-hand punch to the belly. As he fell I stepped around him to face Van Bokkelen.

"You're a damn fool," I said to him. "You'd have to shoot that to stop me, and that would bring the town. If you're going out of here, you'd better ride."

He hesitated, then he laughed. "Why, sure! I never expected you to make so much sense, Pike. You were always such a lily-livered fink."

"Van Bokkelen," I said, "one of these days, when they have that rope around your neck, you think back to this moment. I may never have an awful lot, but I'll live my life out, eating good food, breathing the fresh air, taking a drink now and then, being married to a fine woman, and seeing my youngsters grow up.

"And you? You'll have a fat roll of greenbacks from time to time, and years in prison to pay for it, and always the fear that the next step you make will be the wrong one.

"Back there in jail you said they only wanted you for rustling. Fargo told me they wanted you for murder . . . somewhere back east.

"You can run out of here, and out of the next place, and after a while, even if you're lucky, you're going to run out of places to run to. And then the law will catch up to you."

"The law?" Van Bokkelen said contemptuously. "I never saw a lawman I couldn't out-figure, Pike. Not one. I'm smarter than any one of them."

"Maybe . . . but are you smarter than a hundred of them? A thousand of them? They've got numbers, and they've got time. You haven't got either."

Bohlen started to get up and I moved into position where I could slug him if he tried it.

"I'm keepin' him," I said. "You goin' to argue about it?"

Van Bokkelen looked at me oddly. "You damn fool," he said. "I'm holdin' a gun."

Bohlen hadn't the strength to make it, and he sagged back on the floor.

"That's right, you've got the gun," I said, "and you've got time for one shot before I get to you. Your kind always has the idea that a gun makes the difference. I saw a man take four slugs from a gun like that, and kill the man who was shooting it. Want to gamble?"

"No," he said frankly, "I'll be damned if I do. Here I stand wasting time when I should be riding." He paused. "You going to set the law on me? You going to tell them now?"

"Why should I? You're behind the eight-ball, Van Bokkelen. You're running down a blind trail. No, I'm not going to tell them any sooner than I have to. You make your run—you ain't going any place."

He led the horse to the door and stepped into the saddle. For a minute he looked back at me. "You beat the devil, Pike. I never saw anybody of your kind."

He rode off and I watched him go, and then I went back to where Bohlen was trying again to get up.

He looked up at me like a whipped dog, all the bombast and bluff gone out of him. "You busted my ribs!" he moaned.

"I figured on it."

When the jail door shut on him, the jailer said, "Did you see the other one? The big blond man?"

"He's gone."

The jailer looked at me, saw the fresh blood on me and the bruises. "He gave you no trouble?"

"Only this one. Van Bokkelen . . . him and me, we talked some."

Tired, I walked slowly up the empty street, my footsteps sounding on the boardwalk. But for the first time I walked without being alone. Seemed strange, looking back on the past, that all my life I'd been riding alone and walking alone. The reason was, I'd nobody to do for. What a man needs in this world, if he's any kind of man, is somebody to do for, to take care of. Otherwise there's not much sense in working.

A few lights glowed from windows. Here and there dark, empty windows looked lonesomely at a man. But I had a girl, I had a place to go, and I never was going to be quite so alone again, no matter what happened.

I'd been walking toward the hotel, and just as I neared it I saw a dark figure standing there in the shadows—a strange, bulky figure, looking up at a hotel window. My eyes were used to the darkness, and I could make out the mule, standing there waiting.

"Hello, Lottie," I said. "This is Pike. We talked back on the trail."

"I recall."

"Lottie, that was Philo's sister out there, his sister Ann."

She didn't speak for a few minutes, and then she said, "He was a kind man. Do you suppose he liked me?"

"I'm sure he did, Lottie. You're a nice girl."

She moved out onto the walk, facing me. She was as tall as I was, and looked heavier in her bulky man's clothes.

"What am I goin' to do, Mr. Pike?" Her voice was puzzled, wondering. "Clyde, he used to always tell me what I should do, but he's been dead a long time, and then Mr. Farley, he told me." She peered at me. "I never had no case on him, Mr. Pike, only he talked nice to me, like I was a lady. Nobody ever done that before, not even Clyde. What am I goin' to do, Mr. Pike? I got nobody."

"Lottie," I said, "I'm not the one to ask, but if I was you I'd ride clear away from here, ride some

217

place where they've never heard of Clyde Orum. Then I'd get myself some proper woman's clothes and get myself a job."

She sighed deeply. "I reckon . . . but what could I do?"

"Can you cook?"

"Yes, Mr. Pike, Clyde always said I was the best cook he ever knew. Mr. Farley liked my things too, so I taken them to him. Only when I saw her there, well, I hated her. When a man has his own woman around he don't have time for no big old girl like me."

"Ride out of here, Lottie, get some clothes, and hunt a job as a cook. Don't tell anybody anything about yourself. If you can cook well enough, they won't ask anything else."

"Thank you, Mr. Pike." She turned toward the mule.

"Have you got any money, Lottie?"

"No, Mr. Pike. I ain't had no cash money in a long time."

There wasn't much in my pocket. I never had much my ownself, but Justin had paid me off out there, and a man in jail has no chance to blow it in. And I hadn't spent much since, except to pay Charley Brown what I owed him.

"Lottie, here's twenty-eight dollars. You get yourself out of here. It ain't much, but it's all I've got."

She took the money and stood silent, and then

218

she said, "Mr. Pike, I was goin' to kill that girl. I was fixin' to shoot her."

"I know you were." I paused. "I'm going to marry her, Lottie. Philo wanted it that way."

She stood there for a moment, then walked heavily to her mule and I heard the saddle creak as she got up.

"Lottie," I said, "did you put Indian shoes on your mule?"

"Yes, Mr. Pike. I done that."

"Don't do it again, Lottie. That's all over now. You ride out of here, Lottie, and you be a good girl. There's lots of men who like a big girl who can cook real fine. Especially," I added, "if she keeps herself nice. Neat like, and clean. And keeps her hair combed. You'd best do that, Lottie."

"Yes, sir, Mr. Pike. I'll do that."

She rode away then, and it seemed to me she sat up a little straighter. Or maybe that was just what I hoped.

Standing there, listening to the hoof-falls as she rode away, I thought there wasn't much difference between the two of us after all. Only I'd found the way I was going, and now maybe she had, too.

I turned around and started toward the hotel, where I'd be sleeping that night.

Well, now, let's see. I'd have to make a deal with the Crows about that land back up against the mountain, or find a place just out of their country. A place with plenty of good water, some high meadows where there'd be hay to cut or late summer grazing. Then I'd need a hand to help me round up those cows.

But that could wait. I was a rancher now, a man with stock, and my credit had always been good. First off, I was going to get myself a new outfit of clothes, some that really fit me proper.

What was it Eddie called it? . . . A front.

About Louis L'Amour

"I think of myself in the oral tradition—as a troubadour, a village tale-teller, the man in the shadows of the campfire. That's the way I'd like to be remembered—as a storyteller. A good storyteller."

IT IS DOUBTFUL that any author could be as at home in the world re-created in his novels as Louis Dearborn L'Amour. Not only could he physically fill the boots of the rugged characters he wrote about, but he literally "walked the land my characters walk." His personal experiences as well as his lifelong devotion to historical research combined to give Mr. L'Amour the unique knowledge and understanding of people, events, and the challenge of the American frontier that became the hallmarks of his popularity.

Of French-Irish descent, Mr. L'Amour could trace his own family in North America back to the early 1600s and follow their steady progression westward, "always on the frontier." As a boy growing up in Jamestown, North Dakota, he absorbed all he could about his family's frontier heritage, including the story of his great-grandfather who was scalped by Sioux warriors.

Spurred by an eager curiosity and desire to broaden his horizons, Mr. L'Amour left home at the age of fifteen and enjoyed a wide variety of jobs including seaman, lumberjack, elephant handler, skinner of dead cattle, miner, and an officer in the transportation corps during World War II. During his "yondering" days he also circled the world on a freighter, sailed a dhow on the Red Sea, was shipwrecked in the West Indies and stranded in the Mojave Desert. He won fifty-one of fifty-nine fights as a professional boxer and worked as a journalist and lecturer. He was a voracious reader and collector of rare books. His personal library contained 17,000 volumes.

Mr. L'Amour "wanted to write almost from the time I could talk." After developing a widespread following for his many frontier and adventure stories written for fiction magazines, Mr. L'Amour published his first full-length novel, *Hondo*, in the United States in 1953. Every one of his more than 120 books is in print; there are more than 300 million copies of his books in print worldwide, making him one of the bestselling authors in modern literary history. His books have been translated into twenty languages, and more than forty-five of his novels and stories have been made into feature films and television movies.

His hardcover bestsellers include *The Lonesome Gods*, *The Walking Drum* (his twelfth-century historical novel), *Jubal Sackett*, *Last of the Breed*, and *The Haunted Mesa*. His memoir, *Education of a Wandering Man*, was a leading bestseller in 1989. Audio dramatizations and adaptations of many L'Amour stories are available on cassettes and CDs from Random House Audio publishing.

The recipient of many great honors and awards, in 1983 Mr. L'Amour became the first novelist ever to be awarded the Congressional Gold Medal by the United States Congress in honor of his life's work. In 1984 he was also awarded the Medal of Freedom by President Reagan.

Louis L'Amour died on June 10, 1988. His wife, Kathy, and their two children, Beau and Angelique, carry the L'Amour tradition forward with new books written by the author during his lifetime to be published by Bantam.

Center Point Publishing

600 Brooks Road • PO Box 1
Thorndike ME 04986-0001 USA

(207) 568-3717

US & Canada:
1 800 929-9108
www.centerpointlargeprint.com